Whistling Librarian

Whistling Pines Mystery Book 10

Dean L. Hovey

With Anne Flagge

Print ISBNs

Amazon print 9780228635833
Ingram Spark 9780228635840
Barnes & Noble 9780228635857
BWL Print 9780228635864

Copyright 2025 by Dean L. Hovey and Anne Flagge
Editor S. Peters Davis
Cover artist Michelle Lee

This book is a work of fiction, a product of the authors' imaginations. Any resemblance to actual events, people, or locations is coincidental and unintended. Some actual locations are used fictionally.

"Be the dumpster fire that lends light to the darkness."

— Anonymous

"I hate to hear you talk about all women as if they were fine ladies instead of rational creatures. None of us want to be in calm waters all our lives."

- Jane Austen

Dedication

To Dad, who always thought I could do this.

And to Dean, who also thought I could do this, and let me try. – Anne Flagge

Acknowledgements

A special thanks to Brian Johnson, whose zany suggestions helped us develop the plot, create the characters, and add seasoning to the boiling cauldron of ideas. Madeline Jarvis and Emily Savageau offered Two Harbors Library history and details, which added texture to the story. Paula Pettit, who won the 2025 Two Harbors Library summer reading challenge, earned a cameo as the assistant librarian. As always, there is a legion of additional people who contributed to the book. Deanna Wilson edits the first draft. Julie continues to endure Dean's distracted writing while she keeps the house and family together. David Telker, Mary Telker, and Andy Flagge made suggestions that added depth to characters. Natalie Lund, the sentence structure and preposition rule enforcer, marks up a later draft and improves the readability of the book. Fran Brozo and Clem MacIlravie catch plot issues and correct details specific to their background and experience. Anne Flagge and Mary Telker made a final post-editing sweep to catch the last typos, punctuation errors, misspellings, and truncated words. Without their dedicated assistance, the books would be much less than they are. Finally, thanks to J.D. Shipton, Jude Pittman, and the BWL editors for your contributions and continued support.

Table of Contents

Prologue 9

Chapter 1 11

Chapter 2 21

Chapter 3 39

Chapter 4 50

Chapter 5 65

Chapter 6 85

Chapter 7 96

Chapter 8 115

Chapter 9 128

Chapter 10 141

Chapter 11 152

Chapter 12 170

Chapter 13 179

Chapter 14 195

Chapter 15.. 210

Epilogue..228

Prologue
April 22, 1976

Pushing the car was more difficult than she thought it would be, but with one final shove, she was able to muscle it over the edge of Lafayette Bluff. She was shocked to see the car burst into flames as it tumbled onto a ledge at the bottom of the cliff. Her brother called Pinto cars "the barbecue that seats four." He was right; the car could've burst into flames in an accident and killed her. Seeing it burn and slide, coming to rest on the frozen lake, she watched as the ice melted, then walked away. Destroying her beloved Pinto was painful but this was the only way she could get away from her home and be free of the judgement and shame she would bring to her family. It was better to let everyone think she was dead.

After walking along Highway 61 for a few miles in the dark, she was surprised by the headlights behind her. As the semi stopped for her outstretched thumb, she was happy to see that the person in the seat appeared only to be a few years older than her. He smiled and asked her name. When she replied, "Beth, just Beth," he responded with "Jack, Jack Endicott."

After a few minutes in the truck, he asked, "You have anything to do with that fire back a few miles?"

Grimacing to herself, she responded, "What fire?"

Endicott chuckled. "Where are you headed, 'just Beth?'"

Beth stared out of the windshield, stumped by the question. *Where am I headed? How far away is far enough?* "Where are you headed, 'Jack, Jack Endicott?'"

"I've got a load of pumps for Thunder Bay. I could drop you at any of the towns along the way."

"Let me think about that."

Chapter 1

Today

Two Harbors librarian Madeline Jarvis was reshelving returns when she dropped a book. The sound echoed like an explosion through the library's lower level, startling the fourth graders and parents who were researching science projects. She chuckled and thought, *I need to shush myself.*

Her thoughts were interrupted by the door alarm going off at the library's original entrance, now used only as an emergency exit. Approaching the children and parents, she asked, "Do we know who opened the emergency exit?" The parents and kids looked at each other, all shrugging.

Paula Pettit, the assistant librarian, shook her head. "I don't think anyone went upstairs. All of the students and parents are here. Maybe it's the ghost."

Dashing up the steps, Madeline looked around the older part of the library, revealing an empty room. She got goosebumps as she glanced around the open area, then down the shelves. She wished she'd never heard the story one of the library board members told her about the old section being haunted. After walking down the half-story of steps and re-latching the emergency bar, the alarm stopped. A usually secure door stood ajar below her. She walked down to the archives, where the old newspapers and high school yearbooks were stored. There was no one there either, but she noticed an open drawer in one of the old wooden library tables. Knowing the locked drawer didn't have a key, she was intrigued to find it open. Opening the drawer revealed damaged wood and a broken lock mechanism. The interior of the drawer was dusty and littered with wood chips, except for a clean square in the dust and an adjacent dust-free spot where a folded or torn sheet of paper had been removed.

"I wonder who set off the door alarm?"

Startled by the voice behind her, Madeline turned and found Deb Stone peeking into the room. "Um, someone broke the lock on this drawer."

"What was inside?" Deb asked as she walked over to inspect the damage.

"It's been locked since I started here. My predecessor told me there wasn't a key for this lock. She joked that it probably contained a note from Andrew Carnegie."

"Why Andrew Carnegie?"

"His donation provided the funds to build this library and stock the shelves with books. We joked that the drawer was rather like a time capsule."

"That's right! I'd forgotten about Carnegie's library philanthropy. Old Andrew apparently felt guilty about making millions of dollars and spent his later years building Carnegie-Mellon University, Carnegie Hall, The Carnegie Museum, and funding hundreds of libraries to educate Americans." Deb paused, then asked, "Do you think there was a note from Carnegie in the drawer?"

Madeline stepped back to allow Deb to look inside. "Whoever broke into the drawer removed its contents. The patterns in the dust make it look like there was something square and maybe a torn sheet of paper that could've been a note."

"Interesting. Something square, but very flat," Deb observed. "The drawer is only a couple inches deep. Do you suppose it was a book?"

"There aren't many square books. I was wondering about a music or jewelry box."

"Why would they be in a library drawer?"

"I don't know. They were the only square flat things that came to mind." Madeline reached out to close the drawer, but Deb stopped her. "Don't touch it," Deb said as she took out her cell phone. "Is anything else missing?"

Madeline appeared confused as she looked around the room. "I don't think so. Everything else seems to be in order."

When her call connected, Deb said, "I'm at the library and someone broke into a desk and stole something. Since I'm sure you have nothing better to do, why don't you come over and take a look."

Madeline looked perplexed as Deb ended the call. "Who did you call?"

Deb smiled and extended her hand. "I'm Deb Stone. The police chief is my husband. He's on his way."

"You called the police about a broken library drawer?"

Deb chuckled. "It's probably the most exciting call Kerry will have this week. He'll get to use his fingerprint kit and everything."

Madeline frowned. "That seems a little excessive."

"Weren't you involved in tracing the treasure map found inside the Whistling Pines piano?"

Madeline's eyes lit up. "I was! Do you think there was another treasure map in this drawer?"

"Probably not. But someone was interested enough in the contents to pry the drawer open and steal whatever was inside it." Pulling out two chairs, Deb suggested, "We might as well get comfortable. It's going to take Kerry a few minutes to get here. Do you think this table looks as old as this part of the building?"

"It was probably part of the furniture acquired when the library was built in 1909. The original building was proposed by the city council and mayor as a cultural alternative to the twenty-two bars that were the primary recreational opportunities in Two Harbors until the library opened."

"There were twenty-two bars here?" Deb asked. "I suppose the town was divided into two social groups—the bar patrons and the church people."

"I'm not from Two Harbors, so what I've learned has been gleaned from the historical documents I've read. The town was split in many ways. The original settlers were Norwegian fishermen, who were followed by Swedish immigrant farmers. Each ethnic group built their own church and frequented the ethnically segregated bars."

Laughing, Deb said, "It sounds strange to hear the term segregation when describing Scandinavian groups. I suppose the Swedes went to the bar with the Swedish bartender. And the Norwegians went to their own bars."

"I was told the Swedish and Norwegian Lutheran Churches conducted their services in their home languages into the 1960s. That language barrier segregated the membership very distinctly."

Deb patted the top of the wood library table. "This is solid, unlike anything we'd buy today. Do you think this table migrated down from the original part of the building?"

Madeline pointed to framed photos on the walls. "In these old pictures, there's a table like this in the corner, behind the circulation desk. It held returned books before they were returned to the shelves. I assume the table was moved downstairs at some point after the new addition was built."

Looking around, Deb frowned. "Isn't this room usually locked? I mean, people aren't in here routinely, right?"

"There are fragile old newspapers and yearbooks in here, so I usually keep it locked unless someone's doing research, or we've got a program."

"Did you unlock the room when you came in today?"

"No, the door was ajar, which is why I looked inside when I shut off the alarm. I saw that the chairs had been moved away from the table, so I walked in to put them back when I noticed the open drawer. You came in a moment later."

The main entry door opened in the other room, and someone spoke to the assistant librarian. A moment later, the police chief walked in carrying an aluminum suitcase. Seeing Deb and Madeline, he asked, "Is this the scene of the crime?"

Deb gestured toward the side of the table opposite where they were seated. "The drawer has been pried open."

Pulling on purple gloves, Kerry knelt and inspected the open drawer. "Is this how you found it?"

Madeline nodded. "Someone set off the emergency exit alarm. After I reset the alarm, I noticed the open door and saw the open drawer."

"When did you last unlock the drawer?"

Madeline looked at Deb, then back at Kerry. "Um, to be honest, I'd forgotten there was a drawer in the table. I vaguely recall Margaret, my predecessor, mentioning the locked drawer when explaining the keys I inherited. She said there wasn't a key for the library table drawer."

"So, it's been locked for years?"

"As far as I know," Madeline replied.

After taking a few photos, Kerry commented, "Based on the amount of dust inside, I'd guess it hasn't been open in decades. Do you have any idea what was in the drawer?"

Madeline shook her head. "Like I said, it's been locked the entire time since I took over as the librarian. I haven't seen any notes about the contents of any of the library's drawers. Most of the records I've found pertain to the books or collections of historical items, like newspapers and old high school yearbooks. Your wife and I were brainstorming about square books and jewelry boxes."

"Based on the disturbed dust, it appears something the size of a half sheet of paper was removed, and another torn sheet had been next to it."

"That's what I thought," Madeline replied.

Deb smirked and said, "Maybe it was another treasure map, like the one inside the Whistling Pines piano."

"Please don't propagate that rumor," Kerry said as he stood and took in the table and the surrounding area. "There are wood chips on the floor. When was the room cleaned last?"

"We keep it locked unless we've got a program, so there's no need to sweep the floor most weeks. I suppose it was swept two weeks ago? The janitor might know."

"That doesn't narrow the timeframe much. I don't suppose the thief left his screwdriver and driver's license behind," Kerry joked.

"Not that I found," Madeline replied.

He moved opposite the windows and knelt down to look at the lacquered surface of the table. "There are thousands of fingerprints on the tabletop. Parsing out which belongs to you, the staff, your volunteers, and the people who've done research or attended recent programs will take weeks."

"We do a lot of children's programs here."

"That would explain the chocolate smudges."

Madeline blushed. "I thought we'd cleaned all those up after our S'mores adventure."

"I thought S'mores were a campfire thing," Deb said.

"We used marshmallow cream. The kids had a great time."

Deb gestured toward the suitcase. "Aren't you going to lift fingerprints?"

Kerry looked around the ceiling. "You don't have security cameras?"

"Not in here," Madeline replied. "We've never seen the need for them. There's old stuff in here, but not much of monetary value."

"Unless someone broke into the library, the damage to the lock is vandalism. There are a thousand fingerprints on the table. And whatever was in the drawer had been there for decades. I'm inclined to write it off as vandalism by persons unknown."

Deb gave Kerry a disgusted look. "What else do you have to do?"

"At this point, taking a nap would be a higher priority. On the other hand, if we knew the value of the property taken, I might be willing to spend the time and effort to collect and process the fingerprints."

At a loss for words, the librarian replied, "I just don't know what was in the drawer. If it was something valuable, I assume someone would've opened the drawer long ago."

Kerry's eyes lit up. "Madeline, you know Peter Rogers, right?"

"Yeah. He brings in his senior citizens once a week, and he led the treasure map hunt last year."

"Give Peter a call and have him query his residents about what might've been hidden in the drawer. Who knows, one of the old-timers might remember placing a time capsule or something in the drawer."

After the Chief left, Madeline pulled Peter's number up on her cell phone from the contacts she'd entered during the treasure hunt. Feeling a bit sheepish when Peter answered the call, Madeline blurted out, "Chief Stone told me to call you for help."

"Okay. Who is this?"

"I'm sorry. This is Madeline Jarvis, the city librarian. We had a break-in, and Chief Stone felt you might be able to help me determine what was stolen."

"Why would I know what was stolen?"

Madeline composed herself and backtracked, explaining the locked drawer, the alarm going off, discovering the open drawer, and finding evidence that something was missing from inside the drawer. "That drawer has been locked forever, and I don't have a key for it. Chief Stone thought one of the Whistling Pines residents might remember a time capsule being placed in the drawer...or something."

"I'm busy right now. Would it be okay if I finished up what I'm doing and contacted Chief Stone to get a better understanding of what he had in mind?"

"Take as long as you want. The drawer has been locked forever, the contents are gone, and nothing is going to change between now and whenever you get here."

Chapter 2

When Kerry and I arrived the following day, he asked, "Madeline, are you sure there's nothing more you remember about last night?"

"I'm sorry, Chief. I was so surprised by the alarm going off, I didn't even realize anything was wrong until I went back downstairs to investigate."

I searched the ceiling for a security camera, as Kerry had the night before. "Can we look at the security camera recordings to see who was in the library?"

"Our cameras only cover the lower level, and they've been down since the last thunderstorm. Sparky hasn't been able to get them up and running yet. Paula and I have been wracking our brains to remember who came in last night. It was a little busier than usual as Mrs. Christen's fourth graders have a huge science project due tomorrow, and several students were here doing last-minute research, so we were overrun with fourth graders, frazzled parents, and their excited younger siblings who couldn't be left home alone. Honestly, I was a little stressed myself trying to figure out how vinegar and baking soda react to make a volcano, and Paula was trying to get home to her dog, Flora, so we were both pretty distracted."

Smiling to himself as he pictured the chaos, Kerry responded, "Well, if you think of anything further, let Peter know. He'll have more time to focus on this than me."

"Thanks, Chief Stone. I appreciate your help. Thankfully, nothing seems to be missing from the rest of the library. I can only imagine what might have been in the drawer that was so important to anyone."

I watched Kerry go, then Deb Stone joined Madeline and me at the checkout desk. "I guess I'm in charge of the investigation. I'm not sure what else needs to be done."

"Do you want to check out a book on fingerprinting?" Deb suggested with a smirk.

"Even if I had the vandals' fingerprints, I'd have nothing to compare them to."

"How are you at making vinegar and soda volcanoes?" Madeline asked. "I've got a couple of kids who are struggling. Deb and I are about up to our eyeballs."

I checked my phone for text messages and missed calls. Seeing none, I replied, "Take me to a volcano."

Deb led me to an area where they'd spread plastic on the floor to protect it from paint, papier mâché, and overflowing "lava". Four children and one harried parent were building and painting their volcanoes. Deb handed me a plastic apron, then tied one on herself.

After an hour of leaning over the table, I was relieved when the lone parent announced it was time to clean up and leave. I washed my hands in the bathroom, taking care not to slop paint onto the floor. I met Deb in the hallway outside of the bathroom, where she thanked me for the rescue.

"I didn't know you were a library volunteer, Deb."

After making sure no one was listening, she replied, "I enjoy volunteering here. It's a nice break from my routine. Now that Jacob is getting older, I have more time to do things like this."

"Jeremy and Jacob are at that in-between age where they want to be treated like adults, but they're not quite old enough to understand the responsibilities."

"We're struggling a bit with Jacob," Deb offered. "He wants to be independent and thinks he can be left alone at home. I'm just not comfortable with that yet. How are you dealing with Jeremy?"

"We've got the same issues. He wants his independence, but we are trading bits of freedom for work around the house. I've told him he has to behave like a mature, contributing member of the household before we trust him alone in the house." I paused, then added, "It's not just him being alone that worries me. I don't know how he'd deal with strangers. Our community is pretty insulated from a lot of big-city issues. And this is all new for me."

Deb nodded, then said, "You've never been through the baby and toddler stages before either. Are you handling it okay?"

"I've got to be honest; the lack of sleep was getting on both Jenny's and my nerves for a while. Amy sleeps through the night now, but it's a mad rush in the morning and evening. I'm really exhausted when we fall into bed."

Deb's phone rang and she looked at the screen. "Well, speak of the devil, Jacob is calling, probably wondering where I am."

* * *

Because of my library stop, I was late getting my first cup of coffee in the Whistling Pines dining room when Karla Telker waved at me. She pointed to the open chair at their table. Her usual dining partners, Mary Gilbert and Kathy Christensen, smiled as I approached.

"What's up, ladies?"

Kathy raised her eyebrows and said, "We've been upgraded to ladies."

"You are ladies," I replied.

Kathy, who had a bit of a devilish streak on occasion, cocked her head. "Sometimes it's fun to not be a lady. Constantly behaving yourself is tiring."

"Karla told me she was at a point in her life where she was avoiding drama."

"I don't mind drama, as long as I'm the one who creates it," Kathy replied, her eyes twinkling.

Mary shook her head. "Kathy, I thought your days of drama were behind you."

"You just never know when a bit of drama might spice up a dreary day."

"We heard you were investigating a break-in at the library. What was stolen?" Karla changed the subject.

"No one knows. An old drawer, without a key, had been pried open. There were a couple of spots in the dust that looked like something had been removed, but it wasn't obvious what was gone."

"Ooh, a mystery."

"I don't suppose any of you know what might've been locked in the library table drawer?"

All three women shook their heads. Kathy leaned close to me and whispered, "I spent more time with my boyfriend than I spent in the library."

I looked at Karla. "What? My family was very religious. We didn't play cards, go to dances, or drink liquor."

"That left lots of time to go to the library," I suggested.

"The church library was about as close as I got."

"Mary?" I asked.

"No way. My mom had me practice piano for hours a day. I never had time to go to the library."

Standing, I kidded the ladies. "Well, you three have been no help at all."

Bingle, the janitor, was cleaning up stray bird feathers from around the aviary. "Don't you also clean the library?" I asked.

Pausing to look at us, he replied, "Ya, I do, once a week."

"What do you know about the locked drawer in the library table?"

"The one with no key?"

"Yes, that's the one."

Looking embarrassed, he replied, "A guy asked me if I could get it open."

"And?"

"And I used a screwdriver and opened it."

I stared at him in disbelief. "You're the one who pried open the drawer?"

"Ya, sure, I did," he replied in his heavily accented English.

"What did you find inside?"

"Oh, heck. I got distracted by the door alarm. I need to go back and clean up my mess."

I drew a breath, something I did often to keep from snapping at residents. "What happened to the items you found in the drawer?"

"I think that stuff is still in the pocket of my library coveralls."

"Did you know the guy who asked you to open the drawer?"

"I've never seen him before. He was in the library looking at the table and was going through a big ring of keys, like he was trying to find one that fit the drawer. He asked me if I could open the drawer, so I did. Next thing I know, there's a loud bang like a gunshot, he's gone, and the door alarm is going off. I took out the stuff, assuming he'd be back for it."

"Did he seem to know what was in the drawer?"

"I think so. He said that table had belonged to his grandparents, and it was donated to the library when they died. He was living in Las Vegas and didn't come back for their funerals."

"What was in the drawer?"

Bingle rolled his eyes. "It is stupid. A box. The label says Scotch." When I didn't react, Bingle repeated it. "Scotch. In a box."

"I don't understand what's stupid about it."

"Scotch comes in a bottle, not a stupid flat box. It's not Scotch. I looked inside. It's a stupid plastic spindle with rotten tape. The tape is so old it's not sticky and turned brown." Bingle shrugged.

Confused by his description, I groped. "Scotch tape was invented here. It's tape. Not Scotch whiskey."

Recognition swept Bingle's face. "Sure, the Scotch tape museum. I get it. But this tape went bad. It's not sticky. Just brown, not sticky tape."

Between Bingle's Swedish accent and poor description, I struggled. A thought struck me, and I found a picture of a Scotch brand cassette tape on my phone. So I showed it to Bingle. "Does it look like this?"

"No. I told you. Square cardboard box. Not a dinky plastic thing. Bigger skinny roll of brown tape."

I searched again, this time finding a picture of a reel-to-reel tape. "Like this?"

Bingle pointed to the screen. "Ya! That! Unsticky tape in a flat Scotch box."

I felt like I'd been arguing with my toddler daughter. "The box is in your coveralls here?"

"No. Library coveralls. In the closet by the mop, broom, and vacuum cleaner."

I checked my watch and saw it was mid-morning. "Can we go there now?"

"I'm working. I can't go until after work."

"Okay, where is the closet with your coveralls?"

"It's behind the stairs."

I took a step toward the parking lot and was struck by an anomaly. "Bingle, where were you when the exit door alarm went off?"

Bingle just stared at me as if he didn't understand the question. "You said you opened the drawer for a stranger. He ran off before he got the box from the drawer. Where were you when Madeline came down and found the drawer open?"

"I think maybe I'm in big trouble. So, I hide."

"Why are you in big trouble, Bingle?"

Bingle seemed to be struggling to find the correct English term for what he wanted to say. "The man, he offered to pay me, if I opened the drawer. The keys don't work, so I get a screwdriver. I think I'll just wiggle it to open the drawer. The man, he grabs the screwdriver and breaks the lock and wood. He broke the drawer and left me holding the screwdriver. I think maybe I'll get fired. So, when Miss Madeline goes running upstairs, I go to my closet and hide."

"You were embarrassed about the broken drawer."

"I thought maybe I could clean up the wood chips, and no one would notice. Then, Miss Madeline and the Police Chief's lady go there, and I know I'm in trouble." Bingle paused, looking at his shoes. "You tell them I'll pay to fix. Okay?"

"I don't think anyone cares about the broken drawer. It's been locked shut for a long time."

"You're good with words. You tell Miss Madeline for me. Okay? Tell her I'm sorry and I will fix it. Okay?"

"I'll find good words to tell her. It'll be okay."

Bingle nodded, then walked away. I rushed to the parking lot and drove to the library.

* * *

Madeline was startled, then angry when I banged through the front door. I'm sure she expected some rowdy kid to rush in. Instead, she confronted me. "Peter. You seem to be in a big hurry."

"I know what was in the drawer and where it is."

Madeline's face lit up. "What was it?"

"Show me where the janitor's closet is located."

She led me past the circulation desk to an unmarked door in the hallway. I stepped past her and turned on the light. Bingle's blue coveralls were hanging from a hook on the back of the door. I patted them and quickly found the square box. When I pulled it out of the coveralls pocket, a scrap of paper fluttered to the floor. I shoved the paper scrap into my pocket and opened the flat white box marked "Scotch® recording tape."

"A reel-to-reel tape?" Madeline asked.

"It appears so."

"Why was that locked in a library drawer?"

"First of all, we now know that the drawer hasn't been locked since the library opened. I think reel-to-reel tapes were popular in the '50s and '60s. I think the tape was locked in the drawer by someone who forgot about it."

"Who broke into the desk?"

I cleared my throat. "I'm on a mission of mercy. Promise me you won't get too angry."

"It's not like anything belonging to the library was stolen or destroyed. We have a broken lock on a drawer that didn't work before."

"A man paid Bingle to open the drawer. He tried to slip the lock open. The man got impatient, took the screwdriver from Bingle, and broke the lock. The man panicked and ran out the door without the box he'd been looking for when there was a loud noise from the library that sounded like a gunshot. Bingle panicked when he realized the drawer was splintered and he was holding the screwdriver. You were coming to reset the door alarm, and Bingle hid in the closet while you and Deb Stone inspected the damaged table. He's afraid you'll fire him because of the damage to the drawer."

Madeline waved off the comment. "There's no discernible damage, and the missing contents have been found. Please tell him I forgive him."

"He'll be relieved. He's a sweet old guy who is always willing to help."

"What do you suppose is on the tape? We have old recordings of vets talking about World War II."

"Do you have a reel-to-reel tape player? We can listen to the recording."

"If the library ever had a reel-to-reel tape player, it was gone before I arrived here. I'm sure there must be one somewhere in the library system if a researcher wanted to listen to or transcribe those old stories. I can send a group email and ask the librarians, although, it might be in Grand Marais or someplace equally remote." Madeline's face lit up. "Bob Dylan is from here. Maybe it's an undiscovered Dylan song!"

"Dylan grew up in Hibbing. It's unlikely he would've hidden a tape that wound up in a Two Harbors library table."

Madeline's mischievous look was funny. "Killjoy."

"My assistant was a UMD student. Maybe one of her university contacts has a reel-to-reel player."

"You will let me know what's on the tape, right?"

I smiled. "I suppose technically, the tape belongs to the library. Yes, I'll let you know what we discover."

"You're so much fun, Peter. The plot always thickens when you show up."

* * *

I checked the Whistling Pines activities schedule and saw the afternoon movie listed. *It's already Thursday!* I thought to myself, appreciating Sherry Vogel, my assistant. She kept the recreation activities on schedule while I was frequently dragged away to community commitments as the Whistling Pines representative to the Two Harbors Chamber of Commerce and Police Department. I found Sherry making popcorn in preparation for showing the movie. I showed her the magnetic tape as residents filtered in for the movie. "Have you seen a reel-to-reel tape player at the University?"

Sherry frowned in concentration. "I don't recall seeing one. UMD moved to CDs or digital storage for everything."

"Is there someone you could ask?"

"Sure. I can call Dr. Blankenship. He's been around forever and might know what dusty equipment might be stashed in a back corner of some closet. He found a microfiche reader for a guy who wanted to read old research papers." Nodding to the box, she asked, "Where did you find this? Is it something from here?"

"It was found in a locked drawer at the public library."

"Do you know what's on it?"

"The box isn't marked, and there's no label on the tape." I thought back to the two bare spots inside the drawer and remembered the scrap of paper falling out of the coveralls. I pulled it out of my pocket and spread the paper on the counter. "This was alongside the box."

"It's music."

"Yeah. That's staff paper with musical notes and lyrics."

Sherry studied the notes. "Do you recognize the song?"

I studied the paper and hummed the notes. "This was torn from a full sheet. This looks like the end of a chorus. I don't recognize a tune with these lyrics."

Sherry's eyes lit up. "Maybe it's an undiscovered masterpiece. An original recording of..." she gestured with her arms, making large circles. "Beethoven or Bach."

"Neither of them wrote songs with lyrics. It's more likely this was hidden by some high school kid."

The Mary, Kathy, and Karla trio walked in as Sherry announced her crazy Beethoven suggestion. Mary, who played the organ for one of the churches for most of her life, looked over my arm at the music. "It's not classical. It's a three-chord progression like the high school garage bands played. The lyrics, about Beth, sound like they were written by a teen."

"There you go!" I replied. "It's a love song written by some high school kid." I held out the box. "That's probably what's on the tape, too. Some lovesick kid singing about his broken romance with Beth."

Kathy nodded. "She probably dumped him or moved away."

Mel Rogers stopped behind Mary. "Someone wrote a lovesick song about Beth?"

I held out the staff paper for him to see.

"I'm not musical, so the notes don't mean anything to me. But there was a girl named Beth who died in a car accident back in the '70s, I think." He paused for a moment, deep in thought. "Something strange happened to Beth and her car. They never found her body. I always wondered if the accident was staged, and her body is buried somewhere in the woods."

Howard Johnson stopped behind Mary and looked at the music. "Where's the rest of the song?"

I held up the box. "It might be on this tape. We won't know until I find a reel-to-reel tape player."

The rattling of Hulda Packer's walker preceded her appearance. People stepped aside like Moses parting the Red Sea, each of them having been bumped by Hulda at one time or another. "This is a big turnout for a movie during an epidemic," she announced as she pushed past the others.

"Epidemic?" Mel asked.

Hulda stopped and gave Mel her hairy eyeball look. "Did you miss the announcement? The apiary flu is here. Peter should be handing out masks and Nair."

Mary Gilbert looked at me and whispered, "Nair?"

Hulda's hearing was poor, but somehow whispers were picked up by her $39 hearing aids. She glared at Mary. "Nair is the only treatment. The store shelves are probably bare because people are buying it up and coating themselves with it."

Alma Kotter walked in behind Hulda, grinning. "I volunteer to be the Nair inspector! I'll make sure everyone has been *fully* covered, especially the hunky men."

Kathy leaned to Karla and whispered, "What hunky men is she talking about? Most of the men here have abs more like beer kegs than six-packs."

"There is no epidemic," I announced. "And there will not be any Nair inspections."

Over her shoulder, Hulda shouted, "Tell Jeri Westfall there's no epidemic! The doctor has tried every medicine in his book, and she's still sneezing! The only treatment left is Nair."

I leaned close to Sherry and whispered, "Start the movie."

As Sherry set up Netflix. I handed out popcorn and helped people to their seats. The movie started, so I dimmed the lights. Sherry and I walked into the hallway and closed the door.

"This apiary flu idea is weird," Sherry said, glancing at the door to make sure Hulda wasn't approaching.

"I don't think anyone is gullible enough to buy into Hulda's eccentricities." As soon as the words were out of my mouth, I realized the obvious incorrectness of the statement.

"I don't think it's a matter of gullibility," Sherry corrected. "It's a matter of who has enough mental acuity to know how wrong Hulda is."

"Please call Dr. Blankenship and ask about the tape player."

Sherry held up her phone. "I've got his contact information pulled up and his phone is ringing." Sherry greeted the art professor I'd met during a tour of the Tweed Art

Museum at the University of Minnesota, Duluth campus. After explaining the tape situation, she asked him whether the University had a functioning unit. Her smile and nod announced the reply. "Thanks! I'll give you another call after I talk to the director and determine when we can drive down."

"He has one?" I asked as Sherry ended the call.

"A former professor recorded all of his lectures on reel-to-reel tapes. They keep the tape player around because grad students sometimes use them to gather background for their research."

"Someone listens to decades-old lectures. Isn't that like...listening to corn grow? I mean, every field has progressed over the last half-century. All of that information must be outdated."

Sherry smiled. "Professor Erickson was an icon of art history. That's one field that hasn't moved an inch in hundreds of years. People are still studying Van Gogh's brush strokes, hoping to determine how he gave depth and character to very simplistic paintings."

"Does anyone actually major in art history?" I asked, tongue in cheek.

Sherry laughed. "I hear it's a great major if you want a job as the assistant recreation director at a senior residential facility."

I patted her shoulder. "It is. Call Dr. Blankenship back and see if we can meet with him in the next few days. My calendar is open."

Sherry shook her head. "Your calendar is open because you dumped everything on me. I have a bingo game tomorrow, and I'm taking a group shopping at the mall on Saturday."

"See if after the bingo game would work for him."

Jeri Westfall hustled up to us. "Did I miss the beginning of the movie?"

"It started a minute ago. You haven't missed much."

Jeri paused with her hand on the doorknob. "What's happening after bingo? I didn't see any other activity listed for tomorrow."

Sherry smiled and said, "Peter and I might be driving down to the Tweed Museum tomorrow."

"What a wonderful outing! I love that museum. Is there a signup sheet?"

Sherry looked at me. "Is it an outing?"

"Why not? Ask your contact if he's got a grad student or volunteer who could guide a group of senior citizens through the museum while we listen to the tape."

Sherry nodded reassuringly at Jeri and said, "I'll post a sign-up sheet and write in your name."

Chapter 3

Mornings at home were always hectic, and both Jenny and I rushed out of the house slightly behind our planned departures. I noticed two people standing next to an unfamiliar pickup truck parked in front of Wendy and Sparky's house. Being a good neighbor, I turned toward the pickup and slowed as I approached the couple, who were embracing.

"Excuse me, are you looking for a particular address?"

The couple disengaged, and I recognized Sparky's mother, who seemed mildly embarrassed about being caught hugging a man in front of her son's house. The man, who had a long, graying beard and worn clothing, smiled, showing crow's feet at the corners of his eyes. "No problem," the guy said, continuing to drape his hand over the woman's shoulders. "I'm just dropping off my date."

"Sorry to intrude. I just wanted to make sure you weren't lost tourists."

"As long as you're not a cop profiling me as a biker, I have no problem with the neighbors looking out for their neighborhood."

As I drove away, I reflected on the man's comments. *Dropping off your date at seven in the morning?*

Jenny dropped Amy at daycare and arrived at Whistling Pines a few minutes after me. I waited by my car while she walked over. "Is something wrong at Sparky and Wendy's house? I saw you talking to the people parked in front of their house."

"The people you saw were Sparky's mother and her friend. He was dropping her off after their date."

Jenny froze. "Dropping her off, as in, the date had just ended?" Without waiting for my answer, Jenny tipped her head back. "Her having a serious boyfriend is going to cause some daycare problems for Wendy and Sparky."

"Especially if she's not getting much sleep."

"You jumped to that conclusion quickly."

"Seriously? You didn't come to the same conclusion?"

Jenny started walking to the entrance. "I wasn't going to say it out loud."

"I didn't realize it was better to think it without actually saying it."

"Shh. We don't need to add any topics to the rumor mill."

I stopped just short of the door. "You're the one who keeps reminding me how small Two Harbors is and how quickly news spreads. Remember when we were dating, and the residents knew what we'd done on our date?"

"Yeah, right down to whether I'd substituted onion rings for French fries." Jenny opened the door. "I need to take report from the night nurse. You should probably check the dining room to see if the news about Sparky's mother has preceded our arrival."

* * *

"Achoo!" The small, dainty sneeze echoed in the great room of Whistling Pines. I looked up from my conversation with Howard Johnson, self-styled 'mayor' of the facility, and saw Jeri Westfall anxiously tucking a tissue up her sleeve. Noting the anxiety on her face, I made a mental note to check back in with her later. And to let Jenny know as well.

"It's not like Jeri to make any kind of scene, let alone sneeze," Howard commented quietly when he noticed my concern. An upper respiratory bug had hit the community hard that past fall, and everyone was on the lookout for new symptoms.

"I know. She's always trying to blend in with the woodwork, it seems."

"Your wife, the Director of Nursing, would be the best person to notify," Howard stated.

"Have you heard any rumors about Wendy's daycare situation?" I asked.

A smile flickered on Howard's lips. "You know I don't delve into the swirling eddy of rumors that fly around here." He paused, then added, "I assume you're aware of something or you wouldn't have asked."

Jeri turned and went to the stairs, presumably returning to the second-floor apartment she shared with her husband, Lee. The Westfalls, a couple in their 70s, were well-liked, if not a bit quieter than the rest of the residents at Whistling Pines. And speaking of quieter, I unintentionally caught the eye of Hulda Packer, one of Whistling Pines' more colorful residents.

"Peter, I told you the apiary flu was back in the building. What are you going to do about it?"

"Well, Hulda, if I'd had anything to do with it, I promise I would have told you first. And I don't know that bees have anything to do with it."

"You did tell me about it. After I told you it was coming. You should have sprayed for it."

"There's a spray for it?"

"Yes, Nair."

"I didn't know a hair removal treatment came in spray form?"

"Yes, Nair. And it isn't for hair removal. It's for apiary flu removal." Looking as annoyed as she always did when I didn't jump to her bidding, she continued, "Jeri has been suffering all this time. I already told you her doctor has tried everything. She won't listen to me about Nair. The apiary flu won't go away until everyone around you has done a Nair treatment. I've already done mine and look at me, healthy as a horse."

Thinking to myself that Hulda wouldn't lower herself to any illness, let alone an "apiary flu," I mused aloud, "Hmm, I'll say you do look quite healthy, Hulda. Of course, I'm not an expert on health. That would be Jenny and the rest of the nurses. I'll talk with Jenny about your cure and see what she says." The thought occurred to me that she'd be bald if she'd done a Nair treatment, so I looked more closely at her hair to determine if it was a wig. Not being a good judge of people's grooming, I just couldn't tell if it was a wig or not. I added it to my mental "questions for others" list.

"You do that, Peter. Jenny has a good head on her shoulders. You're lucky she married you."

Realizing that I'd just been insulted by a woman who believed a made-up illness could be resolved by the use of Nair, I held back a sharp retort that flew through my head. Instead, I calmly replied, "Thank you, Hulda, I consider myself lucky every day that she even looked twice at me."

"I've got to get to my apartment. Since you're not getting the cure, I need to make sure I have enough Nair for everyone."

I shook my head in my mind and nodded sympathetically in real life. Poor Hulda, mixed-up things all the time. Once a spry, terrifying elementary teacher, Hulda was now the center of all things chaos at Whistling Pines.

* * *

"Hulda, you cannot sign up for five spots in the van. You can only sign yourself up," Betty Petersen screeched as I turned the corner.

"If I want to have plenty of space in the van for my friends, I can sign up however I want."

"Ladies, what is going on?" I asked as a crowd started to gather at the bulletin board. Howard Johnson stood on the periphery of the group. His slight nod assured me he would have my back if there was a rebellion.

"Peter, Hulda thinks that she can sign herself up five times on the van for the Tweed tour just so she can have more space," Betty hissed.

"That is not the case, Peter. I'm signing up five times so that I can have four friends in the van with me. I don't want to subject myself to people I don't like."

A momentary thought passed through my mind, *I should've driven to the library with only Sherry and skipped the drama associated with a van of seniors.* Knowing I couldn't put that genie back in the bottle, I

44

steeled myself for another tirade. "Hulda, I'm sorry, you can only sign yourself up for tours. If your friends want to come along, they'll have to sign up for themselves."

"That's ridiculous," she snorted as she swung her walker. Anticipating Hulda's move, most of the residents stepped back, giving Hulda space to maneuver.

Unaware of Hulda's impending exit, Bingle stepped into the gap in the crowd, apparently planning to ask me about the tape. His right shin took the full force of Hulda's walker. He jumped back and started hopping on one foot while letting loose with, "*Har du tomtar på loftet?*" Which, I assumed, didn't translate to, "Darn that hurts."

I saw Howard Johnson cover his mouth to hide his laughter. I recalled a comment he'd made about helping his Swedish grandparents on their farm and assumed that he had picked up enough Swedish to understand Bingle's outburst.

Hulda paused for a moment, giving Bingle her stink-eye. "You sound like one of those Svenska Gotter's when they're speaking in tongues." She pushed past him and made her way down the hallway toward her apartment.

I crossed four lines off of Hulda's reservation. "There you go, Betty. Now you can sign up for the tour."

Shaking her head, Betty replied, "No, Peter. I'm not interested in artwork OR a trip to Duluth. It takes forever to get to Duluth, even with the new expressway. I'm happy to stay here in Two Harbors."

I smiled to myself as Betty swept away. "She made a fuss about Hulda signing up for too many spaces on the van, and she wasn't even interested in taking the tour."

Howard approached me, nodding his head. "Betty is fixated on what's fair, whether she has an interest in what's going on or not."

"What did she mean about the new expressway taking forever?"

Chuckling, Howard replied, "That 'new expressway' was completed in 1967." Bingle limped over to us, and Howard put his arm around Bingle's shoulders. "Are you going to be okay?"

"Ya, I'll be fine. But I'll tell you something, I'm going to put a little salt water on Hulda's wheels."

"Salt water?" I asked.

"Just enough to make them squeak. It'll be like tying a bell on a cat so she can't sneak up on people. I'll be able to hear her coming and get out of her way!" He stomped off without addressing whatever brought him to the group in the hallway.

"Howard, what did Bingle say while he was hopping around?"

"The literal translation is, 'Do you have elves in your attic?'" Seeing that I didn't understand, he added, "Have you lost your mind?"

"Wow! That's appropriate."

* * *

Wendy Plauda-Johnson swept into the Whistling Pines community room with as much aplomb as she could muster. Multiple residents swarmed her, grateful to see her back in the building after she'd been gone on maternity leave.

"Where's the baby, Wendy?" I heard one resident ask.

"What did you name it?"

"Why isn't it here with you?"

"Why are you back at work? You should stay at home now that you're a wife and mother. I'm sure Sparky makes enough so you can stay home."

"It's nice to see you all, too," Wendy quipped. "And the answers are 'at home, Blaze, and because I'm working and I like to work.' I'm not going to lie around at home while some man takes care of me. You all went through the sexual revolution. Why are you saying I should stay home? I don't understand. I thought you burned bras so that women had a choice?"

"BLAZE! You named your beautiful baby, BLAZE! What kind of name is that?" Betty Petersen shrieked.

The rest of the ladies murmured their shock at the name, Betty's gall, and Wendy's reprimand. Normally, Wendy was much

47

calmer in her approach to the residents. Shocked, I started to approach the group.

"Sorry, ladies. I am so sorry. It's been a heck of a day, and I was just so happy to get out of the house that I didn't even think about bringing the baby so you could meet him. My mother just left after having been here for six weeks, and I just HAD to get back somewhere sane." The ladies tittered at her idea that things were sane at Whistling Pines. And as if she had been summoned by the "sane" comment, Hulda turned the corner and saw the group.

"What's going on here? Why am I not invited to these Ladies' Aid meetings anymore? Did you all forget I'm president and supposed to be giving the invite, not being excluded?"

"No meeting today, Hulda," Delores Karvonen replied, and with an impish grin, she continued, "We were talking with Wendy about her new baby. She's just back from maternity leave, and we were all hoping to meet the baby. Ask her what she's named it."

"Well, what did you name the little nipper?"

"His name is Blaze, Hulda."

"Blaze! What kind of name is Blaze! As a baby, he'd be an ember, a spark at best, not a blaze!"

"That's very clever. We named him Blaze because his father is Sparky. Obviously, a spark can start a blaze, no?"

"Very clever, Wendy. A little too clever if you ask me. You must have had help. Was it that new Chatty Gippet program that helped you out with that?"

"Chatty Gippet?"

"Yah, that artificial insemination program they have on computers now, the thing students use to write better papers with. The cheating program thing."

"You mean ChatGPT, Hulda?" Sherry Vogel came around the corner shortly after Hulda and was able to identify the gibberish she was spouting.

"Yes, just what I said, Chatty Gippet."

"No, Hulda. Sparky and I chose Blaze all on our own, no artificial INTELLIGENCE needed."

I chuckled to myself as I walked away in search of my umpteenth cup of coffee for the day.

Chapter 4

Sherry parked the van in the drop-off only zone in Ordean Court, and we unloaded our residents. She was then able to find the single available handicapped parking space near the entrance, quickly parked the van, and rushed into the building just as Hulda used her outside voice to ask, "Where is the toilet? You can't take us on a two-hour drive and not have a potty break."

Sherry rushed to Hulda's side as University students turned to see the load of gray-haired people, the age of their grandparents, standing in the student union atrium. "It was only a half-hour drive, Hulda. The restrooms are this way."

"Does anyone else need to use the restroom before we walk to the museum?" I asked.

Lee frowned. "How long is the walk to the museum? I might need to stop now if it's a long walk." I gestured toward the restroom sign, and Lee nodded and said, "Someday you'll have a prostate the size of a softball and you'll understand."

Sherry waited for Hulda outside the ladies' restroom. "I'll take the rest of the group to the museum while you wait for Hulda and Lee."

Lee nodded as he passed. "Good idea. This is going to take a while."

Sherry clamped her eyes shut and grimaced. After Lee closed the door, she looked at me with pleading eyes. "Is this what I have to look forward to with my father?"

"Does he overshare?"

"Peter, my father is the man who picketed the art studio about their use of nude models."

"You should prepare for frequent uncomfortable medical discussions."

"Great. At work and at home."

As I herded the remaining ladies down the hallway, Karla sidled up to me. "You shouldn't scare her. She's a nice girl and an asset to Whistling Pines."

"I'm not scaring her. I'm sharing reality."

"Reality is scary, especially when you're Sherry's age."

"Oh, look. Here's the museum entrance."

Karla tapped me with her elbow. "Nice deflection."

Dr. Blankenship was speaking with a young female student just inside the museum's entrance. Resplendent in his violet suit, the museum director rushed over to shake my hand. "It's nice to see you again! It's been almost two years."

"Life takes unexpected turns."

Blankenship put his hand on my arm. "You should wear a t-shirt with that quote." He steered me to the young woman who had been swarmed by the residents. "Haley! This is Peter Rogers. He's the person I told you about who helped us solve the mystery of the diptych."

Haley smiled, displaying braces on her teeth. "Nice to meet you."

The director looked behind us. "Didn't my favorite ex-student join you?"

"Two residents needed the restroom. Sherry will be here in a moment."

The director nodded excitedly. "Haley, you'll have to introduce yourself to Sherry. She's one of my most successful art history undergraduates."

Karla cocked her head. "What makes Sherry one of the most successful?"

"She had a job offer before she graduated!"

"But it's not an art history job," Karla countered.

"It's extremely difficult to get a museum job with only an undergraduate art history degree. Most students either go on to get a Ph.D. or they find work outside of the field."

Sherry guided Hulda through the door with Lee a step behind.

"And unlike many of my other graduates, she seems extremely happy with her career."

Hulda stopped a few steps short of the director and stared at him. "Who's the fruit?"

If he was insulted by the phrase, Blankenship didn't show it. "Madam, have you been to my museum before? I'm going to turn you over to my assistant, Haley, who's going to give you a tour."

"Is there wine? We were always served wine at our art class."

Blankenship laughed. "I'm afraid we save the wine for our evening groups. Perhaps you'll have to come back another time."

Haley directed the group to the gallery, leaving Sherry and me with the director. I held out the box with the recording tape. "I understand you have a way to listen to this."

"The tape player is connected to a vintage stereo system in the back. Come this way."

Blankenship led us through a door into a room filled with equipment. The tape player sat on a counter where it appeared he'd just pushed the clutter aside. Wires ran from the player to the back of an old stereo amplifier, which was wired to a pair of dusty speakers. He threaded the tape through the head and attached it to a take-up reel. After turning the amplifier on, he hit play, and the reels turned.

The tape started with a man's voice, maybe a male teen, talking about this being a demo tape of a recent composition, while voices spoke in the background. Someone played a few chords on the guitar, then told the people in the background to be quiet. A drummer counted as he tapped his drumstick on the rim, "One, two...one, two, three, four," and someone started singing. "Only once in a lifetime..."

I was struck by the realization that I knew the song. "This is The Gold Rush hit song, 'Barb.'"

The music stopped, then the person spoke again. "Sorry, I've changed the chord progression." He restarted the song in a different key. After a minute, there was another pause while the lyrics were changed. He restarted and finished the first verse, then started what I recognized as the song's chorus with several voices singing backup.

"Stop and back it up, please."

Blankenship stepped back and gestured for me to operate the machine myself. I rewound the tape a couple of revolutions, then restarted it. "My loving Beth..."

I stopped the tape and stared at Blankenship. "The hit lyrics are, 'My loving Barb'. Do you remember it?"

He nodded. "This is apparently an earlier girlfriend. I wonder what happened to Beth?"

Sherry laughed. "Teen boys change girlfriends more often than they change their underwear. He wrote this to an earlier girlfriend, then changed the lyrics when he hooked up with someone new."

Blankenship shuddered.

"What's wrong?" I asked.

"Teen boys not changing their underwear. Gives me the heebie-jeebies."

As I rewound the tape, Sherry asked, "Do you think one of the band members broke into the table to retrieve this tape?" Her eyes went wide. "OMG. The tape is worth like a billion dollars if it's the original demo tape for this song."

"I don't think the thief's motive was financial. I imagine it was someone trying to retrieve a bit of his personal history."

Blankenship crossed his arms and frowned. "The tape is written to Beth. This song is to Barb. I hate to be crude, but those rock singers had groupies who followed them around. My bet is he adapted the song to the name of the girl of the week. That would give him a lot of leverage to..."

Sherry was entering information into her phone. "Okay, I've found a list of members of The Gold Rush. The other reference to a Barb is for their lead singer, Cliff Silver. His biography says his real name is Robert 'Bobby' Megg-Chelsen? Megchelson...how on earth do you pronounce that? No wonder he changed his name. Anyway, he's originally from Two Harbors, Minnesota, and is currently a resident of Las Vegas. He's been married to Barbara McKenna since 1982. They have three children, Brady, Gwen, and Heather." She looked up from her phone and said, "Maybe Barbara doesn't know about this original set of lyrics."

"It's pronounced *Meg-kell-son*," the professor explained, "Megchelson is a Scandinavian derivation of Michaelson."

I removed the partial sheet of paper from my pocket and unfolded it so Blankenship and Sherry could read it. "This is the last part of the song. In the hit song, the lyrics don't mention Barb until here," I said, pointing to the first line of lyrics on the page.

Sherry nodded. "I bet the lyrics were written by Cliff Silver. He must've ditched the tape and incriminating lyrics when he got serious about Barb. Lucky for him, that was before the song became a hit."

"Only one way to find out. Let's listen to the rest of the tape."

The rest of the tape seemed to prove the theory that this was a recording of a song dedicated to Beth and not Barb, as the recorded song serenaded. The three of us looked at each other in amazement as the recording ended. Sherry quickly pulled up YouTube and found a concert version of "Barb." Listening through that version, it was confirmed that this recording was sung to Beth.

"I wonder where or who Beth is?" Sherry mused.

Something was off. Between the tape and the video clip Sherry played, something didn't seem right. I wound the tape again. "Pull up the video of Cliff Silver playing the song again."

Sherry held out her phone and touched the arrow, starting the video. We listened to the first verse and I had her stop the video. "What's wrong?" she asked.

"Listen to the singer on the tape." I started the tape, and we listened to a younger male voice singing to Beth.

Sherry nodded. "I suppose Cliff was much younger when he recorded the demo."

Blankenship frowned. "I don't know, Cliff's voice is gravelly on the video, like Rod Stewart. Maybe he's shouted the lyrics too many times and it's affected his vocal cords."

"Is there an earlier video of the band on YouTube?" I asked Sherry.

She reentered her search and found half a dozen videos of The Gold Rush. Choosing a recording from 1981, she started the replay.

Blankenship looked at me. "His voice is still gravelly."

When the song finished, I restarted the tape and we listened to the second verse. "That's not the same voice. It's not gravelly, and the timbre isn't right. This is someone else's demo tape."

"Maybe one of the band members actually wrote the song and Cliff claimed it for himself."

I entered a search on my phone. "The internet lists Cliff Silver as the original recording artist and the song's writer."

Blankenship chuckled. "And we all know the internet is never wrong."

"Maybe it was someone trying to steal the song from Cliff by sending in a demo tape before Cliff recorded the song?" Sherry suggested.

I rewound the tape while I thought. "It's more likely that Cliff stole the song, and this tape is the original demo. When he came back to town, he remembered this old demo tape and decided he needed to destroy it."

Shaking his head, Blankenship said, "Do you find conspiracies in every corner, Peter?"

"Not in every corner. However, there's a lot of money on the line when you've written a hit song."

Feeling like I had a secondary mystery on my hands, I turned to the museum director. "Thank you for your time and resources, Dr. Blankenship. It's appreciated. We'd better get back to Haley and the residents so we can return to Two Harbors in time for their supper."

"I'm always grateful you think of me when in need. I enjoy a little bit of excitement and mystery; it keeps me on my toes. Students do that, too, but this is a different excitement."

I called Kerry as we walked to the museum entrance. "Meet me at the library in ninety minutes, and I'll tell you what was on the tape."

"Why not tell me now and let me go home to supper?"

"It's only fair that I share the news with Madeline at the same time."

We were surprised to see all the residents in the hallway outside of the museum, especially since it seemed like someone had rung a school bell, and suddenly, it was passing time in high school. It felt like half of the campus was walking past the museum.

"Haley? Is everyone and everything okay?"

"We're fine, Peter. The ladies wanted a chance to see the students, and I knew that the 2 pm classes were letting out soon, so I helped them all out to the hallway."

"Why on earth are they wanting to look at college students?" Then a thought ran through my mind. "Alma!"

Smiling, Alma said, "Peter, I just wanted to see how handsome these college boys were. It's not been that long since I was their age myself, you know. I was quite a looker back then. The boys all hung on me. Since we're so close to the gym, I was hoping there might be some of those hunky athletes in running shorts walking to class."

"Alma, you are the very definition of staying young no matter your years." I shook my head and tried not to smile as I thought about how these students might react if they knew an octogenarian, who liked to flash crowds of people, was leering at them.

Nodding at Sherry, I announced, "All right, folks, Sherry's bringing the van around, let's thank Haley for her time today and head out. I think it's roast beef for supper tonight, and I know I wouldn't want to be late for that."

That got the residents moving marginally faster, but it still took nearly 20 minutes to get everyone loaded up. The ride back to Whistling Pines was uneventful as it seemed that all the walking the residents did at the museum was enough to lull them into sleep once the van warmed up and was on its way north. Sherry and I talked quietly on the ride back, knowing that we couldn't discuss the discovery but could discuss further plans for the residents' activities.

I checked my watch as the residents exited the bus. "Can you handle this? I'm supposed to meet Chief Stone at the library."

"No problem," Sherry replied. "What are you going to tell him?"

"We have a deeper mystery. The hit song wasn't written by Cliff Silver."

"Maybe someone gave Cliff the rights."

"There would be legal battles. I think it was Kris Kristofferson who said the royalties from a hit song would buy a small town."

"What do you think happened?"

I glanced at Sherry in the mirror. "I suspect that Beth and the songwriter disappeared at the same time, making Cliff Silver rich and famous."

* * *

I told Kerry about our trip to the museum and listening to the demo tape. He nodded and thought as we crossed the street to the library entrance. "Don't mention those thoughts. Let's see if Madeline comes up with a different explanation for the lyric and songwriter change."

Kerry approached the library desk and said, "Madeline, remind me again about the box we found. I'm wondering what thoughts you've had."

"I've been thinking about it too. I have a bit of a mind for words and have memorized the lines on the paper. It sounds like a bit of a poem. I'll enter the lines into a search engine and see what I get."

"Great idea, Madeline, let's see what comes up."

Entering the lines into her search engine, the song came up from The Gold Rush. "The song, 'Barb,' is on their debut album. The band received a Midwestern Music Award, but the song never had much play time on popular music sites."

"But wait, it said 'You're the one, Barb, the one I'm gonna love forever' on the internet and the handwritten lyric is 'You're the one, Beth'..."

"Maybe someone liked the song so much they put their own name into the lyrics?" Madeline suggested.

"Interesting thought," Kerry commented.

Madeline cocked her head. "Peter, were you going to UMD to listen to the tape this afternoon? What was on it?"

"It's apparently an early demo tape of the song, written to a different woman. The voice doesn't sound like Cliff Silver. Were there any other songwriters or poets of note here in the 1970s?"

"Um, none that come to mind. I suppose I could check the old yearbooks to see if anyone was listed as 'most likely to become a famous poet.'"

"Please do that," Kerry urged. "Also note if there were any other garage bands mentioned."

"Even focusing on the 1970s, this might take a while."

I nodded. "Do it as quickly as you can, please."

Madeline's eyes twinkled. "I might not get a chance until after we close. It's quiet and I might get through the yearbooks quickly if I'm uninterrupted."

Kerry urged me toward the door. As we left, he said, "Well, Madeline, if you find anything else or someone remembers the person who came in, let one of us know."

"Will do, Chief Stone. Thanks again for coming so quickly the other night. It was so bizarre. It's good to know we're well cared for in Two Harbors. You're a great asset to our community."

Blushing slightly at the praise, Kerry nodded and turned to me, "Let's head out.

I've got to finish up scheduling for next month before I can go home, and you probably have dinner to make for Jenny and the kids."

"Thanks for the reminder. Can we stop at the grocery store on the way back to my place? I forgot to pick up ketchup on my grocery run last night."

"Of course," Kerry sighed.

Madeline giggled and headed back to her work as Kerry and I left.

As we walked to the parking lot, Kerry asked, "Knowing about the demo tape and what the internet search produced, what's your theory about the song and how it relates to the library break-in?"

"Cliff Silver wants to hide the identity of the original songwriter, or he might know the value of that demo tape and wanted to recover it for sale. Or he doesn't want his wife to know the song was written for an old girlfriend. He wants the tape in his hands. What do you think?"

Stopping at his car, Kerry thought for a moment. "What if Cliff Silver, or whatever his real name is, killed Beth and the songwriter? Back on his home turf, he's afraid someone would connect the dots if they heard the song lyrics with Beth's name."

"Mel Rogers told me about a girl named Beth who disappeared from a car accident in the '70s. Do you think there was a second person in the car?"

"Two bodies disappearing from a crash is unlikely. I think it's probable the songwriter was scared off or died before Beth's disappearance." Kerry looked over his shoulder to make sure no one was following us. "I'm going to look through the '70s reports for teen deaths and missing persons."

I shook my head. "Why do you always drift to the grisliest motives?"

"Unlike you, I see the dark slime under every rock. Two Harbors isn't Disneyland, and we're not on the 'It's a Small World' ride."

* * *

After the children were tucked into bed, I told Jenny about the tape, the unknown singer, and our suspicions about Beth's disappearance being linked to the songwriter. She bit her bottom lip and closed her eyes. "What's going on?"

"I think the someone is trying to tie up loose ends."

"You're digging into this. Does that put you in danger?"

"I doubt it. This is fifty-year-old history. We weren't born yet when any of this happened," I replied.

Chapter 5

The next morning, Jenny asked me to join her on her morning rounds. "I'm a little worried about Jeri Westfall's sneezing spells. I'm afraid she's going to lose her balance and fall."

We reached their apartment just as Jeri and Lee stepped into the hallway. "Jeri, how have you been feeling lately?" Jenny asked as we walked down the hallway toward the dining room, with Lee following two steps behind.

"I don't know, Jenny. Some days I'm just fine, but then other days, I just can't stop sneezing. I can't quite understand what might be going on. I went to the doctor, and she didn't find anything she could treat. I just sneeze and sneeze for no reason at all, then it stops. Come to think of it, I only sneeze here at home. I didn't sneeze once at the doctor's office or at the pharmacy when we stopped to pick up more tissues. I guess I'm just a medical mystery."

"Well, mysteries are right up Peter's alley," Jenny teased.

"I've never looked into a medical mystery before, Jeri, but I'm happy to keep an ear out for anything suspicious," I offered.

"You're such a dear, Peter. I appreciate you so much."

"Happy to help, Jeri."

Jeri continued on a few steps, then sneezed as she passed Dottie Preston's door. Dottie, just stepping out of her room, startled, and responded, "Gesundheit," as Jenny and I said, "Bless you."

"Good morning, Dottie." I can see Jenny making her usual mental assessment of Dottie's physical appearance, somewhat disheveled but healthy-looking. "How is your morning going?"

"It's fine, Jenny. Everything is just fine. Why do you ask?"

"Just saying hi, Dottie. Have a good breakfast."

Dottie stepped back into her room, placed a lint roller on the counter, then rushed to catch up with us after making sure her door was fully shut.

Jeri made her way a few steps ahead and into the dining room. As Dottie power walked past us, Jeri once again sneezed, and Dottie responded with another, "Gesundheit."

I looked at Jenny and smiled. Jenny shook her head. "You just never know what you'll get out of Dottie these days, do you?"

"Absolutely. She's been very defensive lately, Peter. I'm sure she's just having a bad week, but it's hard to have a conversation with someone who seems like everyone's out to get them."

"It's almost like being around teenagers, right? Jeremy is like that some days. One minute, he's happy to have us around, the next, he's asking us to leave him alone. I know it's a phase, but it's frustrating."

"Yup. He's definitely a teenager. Do you remember being a teenager? Life was "so" complicated then. Who's gonna be hanging out? Will my outfit be cool at school tomorrow? Today's a different story. I'm grateful we've never allowed him to have a phone, can you imagine?"

"You're not wrong about Jeremy. So, what do you think? Dottie, the world's first octogenarian teenager, right?"

"Hilarious, Peter."

Oh man, I got the side eye again. Dang, I thought my dad jokes were getting better. I'd better go help Sherry with next month's activity list before I get into more trouble. "I love you, see you at home."

"I love you too."

* * *

While sitting at my desk, I considered Kerry's comments, what I knew, and the questions our discoveries had raised. Brian stepped into my office, interrupting my thoughts. "It looks like you're praying," he said.

"I'm looking for divine intervention."

I could tell by the sparkle in Brian's eyes I'd triggered the memory of a tuba joke. "Did you hear about the minister whose organ broke down on December 24th?"

"No, Brian. What happened?"

"Desperate for Christmas Eve music, he called local bands, all of them were booked or tied up with their families. One band leader offers to make a couple of calls. Minutes before the service was about to begin, the church doors burst open, and an accordion/tuba duo rushed in. The minister was confused and looked behind them. 'Where's the rest of the band?'

"The tuba player replies, 'There's just the two of us.'"

"The minister waves them into the sanctuary, and after a brief introduction, he nods to the musicians who start playing a polka. The minister cringes but sees smiles on all of the parishioners. The concert lasts an hour and includes a couple of Christmas carols. After the service, the minister rushes up to the duo and thanks them. 'That was the best Christmas concert ever! Can we book you for next year?'"

"The two musicians look at each other and shrug. 'Sure, can we leave our instruments here until then?'"

I grimaced.

Thinking I hadn't understood, Brian added, "Do you get it? They don't have another gig before next Christmas."

"Yeah, I got it." Taking an opportunity to move to a more productive topic and hoping to tap into Brian's music background, I asked, "What do you know about a song called 'Beth'?"

"It doesn't sound familiar. Should I know it?"

"The library had a break-in, and someone stole a tape and left behind a half sheet of paper with lyrics for a song named 'Beth.' The song was later released as 'Barb,' and it became a hit."

Brian's gaze drifted to the ceiling above my head as he thought. "Beth was the woman who died in the 1970s car crash on Lafayette Bluff. I was a kid, and that was all anyone talked about for weeks. There were volunteers climbing all around up there, trying to find her body."

"Was she alone in the car?"

"I think so. I don't remember anyone talking about another person."

"Do you remember Beth's last name, or if anyone wrote a song about her?"

"Phew. That was a long time ago, Doc. You might have better luck asking some of your residents who were adults at the time. Maybe one of them was her neighbor or knew her family."

Accepting Brian's reasoning, I replied, "Having a name associated with the car accident may be enough to break the logjam."

Brian stood, then froze. "I came here for a reason."

"Besides telling me the tuba/accordion joke?"

"I usually have a serious reason for bugging you. The jokes are just icing on the cake." Brian paused, trying to bring back his lost thought. "You've distracted me from my mission."

"Like forgetting why you've walked into the next room?"

"Yes," he replied. "It's infuriating."

"Call me if you think of the reason."

Stopping at the door, Brian looked perplexed. "Have you heard of the Secret Owl Society?"

I waited for the punchline, then said, "No."

After closing my door, Brian sat and leaned forward. "I'm not supposed to know about them."

"Are they like the Moose Lodge or Fraternal Order of Eagles?"

"Not at all. They're a close-knit group of owl spotters."

Sensing my leg being pulled, I leaned back. "There's a secret group of owl spotters? Aren't there owls all over the place?"

"You've been out to the Sax-Zim Nature Area, right?"

"Yes, I brought a group of residents there a few years ago."

Brian nodded. "Then you know what a zoo it is. There are busloads of people from all over the world that swarm over the birds and scare them away."

I thought back to the residents rushing to one side or the other of the bus to try and spot and take a picture of the birds. "The Secret Owl Society isn't like that?"

"They text each other when an owl is located. Each member sneaks out to the location where they listen for the owl and wait for Bruce."

"Who's Bruce?"

"Bruce!"

I shrugged. "I don't know Bruce."

"Your barber, Bruce."

I thought back to my last haircut and thought of the array of wildlife pictures that covered Bruce's shop. "Okay, they call Bruce the barber. So what?"

"They don't *call* Bruce. Someone texts Bruce. He grabs his camera bag, and someone picks him up. No names are used. No locations are revealed."

"Brian, this is a little far out, even for you. A cameraman who's spirited away by strangers to an unknown location."

Brian smiled and added, "In the middle of the night."

I closed my eyes. "In the middle of the night?"

"Of course. That's when owls are out."

"Why do these secretive people drag Bruce out to take a picture?"

"Bruce is a pro. He gets world-class pictures the members can display in their owl shrines."

"What does Bruce get out of this?"

Brian's grin made me feel like I'd missed the joke. "Bruce's pictures have been on the covers of every major wildlife magazine. The only constraints the Owl Society put on Bruce are that he does not identify the members, he doesn't reveal the specific location of his pictures, and he doesn't post or publish any picture until ninety days after it's taken."

"You know a lot about this alleged secret society."

"People tell me things because they know I can keep a secret."

I leaned back. "Brian, you have literally told me everything you know about any topic of interest."

Brian blinked. "I'm *extremely* discreet. I tell you things because you're solving crimes. You don't know ten percent of the secrets I know. And I know that you're not a rumor monger, spreading news around."

I glanced at the computer clock to see how much time I'd wasted on the Secret Owl Society discussion. "Is this going somewhere?"

"You're disappointing me, Peter. What's common to all of the deaths you're investigating?"

"Um, they occurred near here fifty years ago."

"They happened at night. And when do people spot owls? At night."

"Brian, what are the odds Bruce would be at a particular spot at the exact time someone was killed?"

"Northern Saw-Whet Owls eat fish. They're small owls, so they eat small fish. Where do we find lots of small fish around Lake Superior?"

"Enlighten me."

"When the smelt are running! The Secret Owl Society members move up and down the shoreline to whichever rivers have the best smelt run. If they hear or see a Saw-Whet owl, they text Bruce."

"I've never heard of a Saw-Whet owl."

"Look it up on your computer." As I logged in, he added, "They're tiny guys, only six to eight inches high, and they're very elusive. It's a big deal to get a photo of one."

I typed in a search, and within a minute, we were looking at a picture of a round-headed owl with oversized yellow eyes. The 'too-too-too-too" vocalization sounded like a truck backing up.

"This seems very unlikely," I said as I turned off the owl video.

"Have I ever steered you wrong, Doc?"

"Are you kidding? I can't even count the number of rabbit holes you've sent me down."

"Call Bruce."

"Can I tell him you gave me his name?"

Brian froze. "NO! Tell him you've seen his photos and wanted to talk about the owl pictures. Don't out me."

* * *

I walked to the Whistling Pines dining room with my coffee mug in hand. Karla stopped me before I got to the urn. "You have to do something about Hulda. The drugstore is going to be out of Nair, and everyone will be bald if she keeps talking about treating the apiary flu." She paused, then asked, "That's not a real thing, is it?"

"It's totally Hulda's twisted memory. I'll have a word with her, although I doubt it will do any good."

Karla leaned close and whispered, "I probably shouldn't say this…"

That intro was usually followed by something Karla should not have said.

"I think Jeri's sneezing is an allergy. The only time she sneezes is when we come down to eat. Maybe she's allergic to one of the residents. See what happens if you move her around to different tables to see who's causing her reaction."

"I've never heard of an allergy to a person. If Jeri's having an allergic reaction, I imagine the cause is *something*, not *someone*."

Seeing the remainder of Karla's tribe, I suggested that we sit with them. "Good morning, ladies," I said as I pulled a chair to their table.

Mary smiled and asked, "Aren't you afraid you'll catch the apiary flu from us?"

"I've been vaccinated."

Kathy's smile was more mischievous. "You've already rubbed Nair all over yourself?"

Ignoring Kathy's smile, I moved on. "I'd like to pose a question to you three. Do you remember a 1970s car accident where a girl named Beth disappeared?"

"Elizabeth Eggleston!" Mary blurted out. "I remember! Her Pinto went over the cliff between Two Harbors and Beaver Bay."

"Do you recall any of the details about the crash?"

"I remember Beth from high school. She drove a Ford Pinto, and they'd just been written up as dangerous because the gas tanks burst into flames if you got rear-ended."

"Was anyone in the car with her when it crashed?"

The three women looked at each other, waiting for someone else to answer. Finally, Karla said, "I think she was alone. No one ever mentioned someone else being in the car with her."

"Did her boyfriend disappear at the same time?"

Karla looked shocked. "I think she'd broken up with someone after the prom."

"Do you remember any songwriters or bands playing in town back in the day?"

"Songwriters?" Mary asked. "Someone whose songs were actually published and played?"

"Or someone who dabbled with it but maybe never had a song published?"

Kathy tilted her head. "Back then, every third guy had a guitar and was trying to sing popular songs. Most of them couldn't master the tough chords like the Beatles or Eagles used, so they sang the simple one-hit-wonders."

"Do you remember any names?"

"Bands called The Accidentals and The Outcasts played at the high school, back in the day."

"How about you, Mary?"

"The Outcasts changed their name." Mary's brow wrinkled as she thought. "I think they became The Gold Rush."

Karla jumped in, "Yes! They got a record contract and had a couple of hits.

* * *

I was watching the seniors gather outside of the dining room in anticipation of lunch when Howard Johnson stepped away from the group and waved to me. "Peter, did you hear that The Gold Rush is having a reunion concert?"

I was struck by the coincidence of the recording tape in the library drawer and the hit band having a local reunion. "Why in Two Harbors?"

"They're four guys *from* Two Harbors who started playing in their parents' garages.

They played for a couple of dances when my youngest daughter was in high school, then they moved on to larger venues in Duluth and Minneapolis before signing a record deal."

"And they're having a reunion here?"

"The bass player and drummer moved back and got real jobs after the band broke up. The lead guitarist and keyboardist are flying back from California and Las Vegas."

Dottie overheard us and stepped closer. "Cliff Silver was hot."

I laughed, "Cliff Silver?"

"That's what the lead singer called himself. I guess the record label didn't think Bobby Megchelsen made a good stage name."

"Where is the concert?" I asked.

"They're going back to their original first concert location, the high school auditorium."

Howard smiled and added, "Not exactly their original venue. That school doesn't exist anymore. They're playing in the new high school."

Karla joined our group and asked, "Are you talking about The Gold Rush reunion?"

Hearing the concert being mentioned, Jeri joined us. "A high school concert by a local band. How fun!" A second later, Jeri sniffled and then turned her head to sneeze. "Achoo."

"Bless you," Karla said. "Are you catching a cold?"

Hulda spun her walker around, banging into my shin. "She's not getting a cold. Haven't you heard that Jeri has the apiary flu?"

Howard grimaced. "I think it's called the avian flu."

"Nope," Hulda corrected. "It's the apiary flu, and the only treatment is Nair." She turned to Dottie and picked a white hair off Dottie's black sweater. "It looks like your sweater could use a Nair treatment."

Dottie blushed, then turned to pick a few hairs off her sweater sleeve. "Excuse me. I need to find my lint roller."

"Poor Dottie. She's been so distracted lately."

"Dottie's been distracted? How so?" I query the group.

"She used to play cards all afternoon with Pixie Kangas, and they haven't played in at least a month." Karla thinks and then continues, "Come to think of it, I think it's been three months since she's participated in much more than the Thursday movies. Strange."

Filing away the information for a future conversation with Jenny, I ask Hulda more about her theory about the apiary flu. "Hulda, tell me more about the apiary flu. I assume since Jeri is sneezing, one of the main symptoms is sneezing?"

"Yes, Peter," she replies with a long-suffering sigh. "I know I've told you all about this at least twice before, pay attention this time. Apiary flu is a virus that can be cured by Nair. None of those fancy anti-bee-otics can do anything for you. You have to use Nair.”

Aha, apiary flu and "anti-bee-otics," now I get the connection. Poor woman. As I think this through, I can see several in the group making the connection as well. Smiling, I thank Hulda for her time and knowledge. Knowing that stroking her ego goes a long way, I ask, “Hulda, you’re always so busy with friends, you must be reading for hours at night, learning new things about the world.”

“Pshaw, Peter. This is all common knowledge, so there is no need to do any reading, other than the newspaper and watching Channel Three news. If you catch the 6 o’clock news, you get all the local information. You know, the national CBS doesn’t know what’s really going on in Minnesota. You have to check with the local news to be really sure.” Stunned at her seemingly lucid argument, I could only nod in amazement as she banged away toward the community room.

Howard joined me as Hulda toddled away. “Are you arranging transportation to The Gold Rush concert?”

“I hadn’t thought about it. I’ll mention it to Sherry.”

“There’s going to be a big crowd. I heard they’re dedicating the concert to Kenny Donaldson.”

"I don't know that name."

"He was the band's original keyboard player."

With my curiosity piqued, I asked, "What happened to him? Did he die of a drug overdose in a Las Vegas hotel like so many rock stars of that day?"

"No, he died locally, before the band became famous."

* * *

I called the library from my desk, and Madeline answered on the second ring. "Did you find a songwriter in the yearbooks?"

It took her a moment to redirect her train of thought. "Sorry, one of the kids just asked me if I'd ever read a book that made me cry."

"What did you tell her?"

"She was about six, so I said, 'Old Yeller.'"

Chuckling, I said, "I think the last book that made me cry was calculus."

"That's not part of a library science curriculum," I heard paper shuffling, then Madeline was back on the phone. "The yearbooks were interesting, although I didn't find any songwriters or poets among the students voted 'most likely to.' There were several downright nasty ones that I'm surprised got past the yearbook advisor/censor. Robert Megchelson was voted most likely to become a famous

80

musician. Aside from him, there really weren't any poets or musicians."

"Do you have the yearbook with Megchelson nearby?"

"Yeah, it's right here. I'd planned to leave you a message later."

"Please look up two names from that class: Kenny Donaldson and Elizabeth Eggleston."

"Peter, the entire 1976 yearbook is dedicated to their memory. They were classmates who died shortly before graduation."

"Does it say anything about their deaths?"

"Not really, just that they're always in our hearts."

"What was Elizabeth Eggleston most likely to be?"

I heard pages turning. "Elizabeth Eggleston, most likely to be the first woman to win the Indianapolis 500."

"I guess she must've had a few speeding tickets. How about Kenny Donaldson?"

"Kenny Donaldson was most likely to become an accountant. I suppose he was quiet and good at math."

"Thanks, Madeline. Call me if you find a songwriter."

* * *

I was shutting down my computer when Wendy rushed into my office. "Oh, good. You're still here."

"What's wrong?" I looked past her to see if someone else was part of her emergency.

"Joey has food poisoning!"

Running through the roster of residents, I couldn't recall anyone named Joey. "Food poisoning is more of a Jenny the nurse problem. Why are you telling me?"

Rolling her eyes, Wendy said, "Joey is our lead guitar player. We've got a gig at Hugo's tonight, and I need you to fill in."

"I can't bail on Jenny and the kids on such short notice."

"Jenny said it was okay."

"You asked Jenny if it was okay before asking me if I'd be willing to play?"

Wendy's Cheshire cat grin always irritated me. "I know who controls the social calendar at your house. We're on at 7:00, so plan on arriving by 6:30 so we can warm up and go over the playlist."

"But..."

"Don't waste my time with one of your cheesy arguments. You *WANT* to do this. You live for the chance to play in front of a real audience. I'll see you at 6:30." She dashed out, then stuck her head back into my office. "By the way, we're doing country rock songs."

Part of enjoying a gig is practicing and building anticipation. Being told to be in a bar in two hours wasn't the kind of anticipation I wanted. That had been replaced with two hours of dread. I had to pull out my guitar and equipment. I had to find clothes...country cut clothes. I had to make sure Jenny and the kids were set for the night. I had to drive to Hugo's, which was miles outside of town, on a road known for deer encounters.

"Shit."

Kerry pulled into the parking lot as I walked to my car. Spotting me, he turned down the row I had parked in and stopped, blocking my car. He leaned against the fender when I reached his stopping spot.

"What's up, Chief?"

"Have you had any more thoughts about the broken library drawer?"

"The thief was probably someone from the rock group that will be playing a concert at the high school. The tape was a demo they'd made long before their hit song was released."

Kerry pushed himself off the fender. "Mystery solved."

"Wait! There's more. The singer on the tape isn't Cliff Silver, the band's lead. And the lyrics are written to a different woman."

"We knew that last night," Kerry said as he checked his watch.

"The band had a different keyboardist back then, and they're dedicating the concert to him."

"That's a nice gesture."

"The guy died before the band had their big hit. Did you see anything about Kenny Donaldson's death when you looked through the old files?"

"Nope."

"Aren't you going to pursue it?"

"If he died outside of my jurisdiction, it falls slightly lower on my 'to do' list than identifying the people who dumped the four tires under the stands at the football field."

Because of his burn scars, Kerry's face was hard to read, but I sensed something unsaid. "You've got something more pressing."

Kerry nodded slightly, unwilling to elaborate, then stepped away from the fender. Understanding I had no need to know what his police priorities were, I nodded back.

"What are you and Deb doing tonight?"

Kerry stopped with his hand on the car door. "I suppose we'll eat supper and watch TV like most nights. Why? Do you have something more interesting for us?"

"I'm filling in for the Gin Fizzes' lead guitarist. We're playing at Hugo's starting at 7:00."

"I suppose that's more interesting than watching reruns. I'll mention it to Deb."

Chapter 6

Wendy bustled into Hugo's, baby bag and Blaze in tow, along with her tambourine.

"What on earth? Wendy, you can't bring a baby into a bar!"

Visibly holding in a deep sigh, Wendy retorted, "I know that, Peter." The "duh" was nearly audible. "Sparky's mom bailed on me, and Sparky is out on a work call. I have little earmuffs for Blaze. He'll be fine."

"She bailed on you at the last minute?"

Wendy paused as if counting to ten. "She has a...male friend."

Feigning ignorance, I gaped, "Sparky's mother has a boyfriend?"

"It's hard to call a guy who looks like Willie Nelson a boy. Let's leave it at she's dating."

Grabbing my phone out of my gig bag, I said, "I'm calling Jenny. I'll see if she can come and get the baby. Blaze and Amy can stare at each other while Jeremy groans about baby smells."

"I can't ask that of Jenny, Peter. She doesn't need to have a third child at home while you're playing with the band."

"I'm sure she'll be fine with it. And if she's not, she'll take it out on me for asking, not you."

Wendy sighed but smiled as the baby cooed at the lights in the bar. "Fine. I'll accept her help if she's willing to take him. Thank you, Peter."

As the phone rang, I smiled at the baby, wishing I could hang out with him with my family instead of playing at the bar. *Babies aren't so bad when there's a lot of help*, I thought as the phone rang.

"What did you forget this time, Peter?"

"Jenny, you have so little faith in me. This time, I didn't forget anything. I'm calling to ask if you can help Wendy out. Her babysitter bailed on her, and Sparky is out on a call. Can you come and grab Blaze and have him hang out with you guys until Sparky gets home?"

"I'd be happy to. I wish she'd have called before she left home, then she wouldn't have had to bring him to the bar at all."

"She wasn't happy I was asking you to do it, to be honest. She figured he'd be fine here with his baby earmuffs. Besides, someone would have probably held him the whole time. There's always someone in the crowd who can't resist time with a baby."

"I'll load up the kids and be there in about thirty minutes."

As I repeated Jenny's request, Wendy nodded and added, "Have her text me when she's outside so you don't have to stop what you're doing, might as well just be me who's interrupted."

I replayed the information, and as I hung up the phone, I glanced at Wendy, who was fidgeting with her gear and the microphone. "Jenny will be here in thirty minutes."

The relief in Wendy's eyes was obvious. "Thank you, Peter. You and your family are lifesavers."

Kerry and Deb walked in and sat at a table a row back from the stage. I nodded at them. Seeing an opportunity, Wendy waded through the crowd and whispered to Deb, who nodded. A moment later, Blaze was sitting on Deb's lap.

Wendy gathered her thoughts for a second, then she smiled at the nearly full room. "Hi folks. We're the Gin Fizzes, and tonight we're going to do our country rock show. I think you'll remember this one made famous by the Allman Brothers, 'Ramblin' Man.'"

The crowd was getting into the song, and the band was in sync. Blaze was less taken with the music than the rest of the crowd, and he started to cry. Deb did her best to quiet him, but Blaze wasn't having it. When the song ended, Wendy whispered to me during the applause. "Play something long." Then, she stepped off the stage and picked up Blaze.

At a loss, I tried to think of a long song. Turning to the bass player I asked, "Do you know Don McLean's 'Vincent?'"

He shrugged. "Play a few bars and I'll follow you."

I smiled at the crowd, and they smiled. "I don't know if this fits the genre." I played the opening and sang, "Starry, starry night, paint your palette blue and gray..."

Wendy bounced the baby in the back through the performance, and he settled down. By the end of the song, the bar was full, and they applauded. I looked at Wendy, hoping she was ready to hand Blaze back to Deb. She shook her head, and I looked at the bassist. "What's next on your playlist?"

"'Hotel California.'"

"Can you sing the harmony?"

His reply was a snort and a headshake. "I'm not the lead singer for a reason."

I looked at Deb Stone and recalled her dragging me onto the stage at the Lutheran Church to sing a duet. "Our next song needs a female singer. Luckily, Deb Stone is in the audience. I'm sure she'd be willing to sing if given a bit of encouragement."

The crowd started clapping, and Deb turned red while glaring daggers at me. I pulled a stool forward and motioned for her to join me. She whispered to Kerry, who gestured toward the stage. Facing away from the audience, she whispered to me. "I'll kill you when this is over."

Covering the mic, I replied, "This is payback. I hope you know 'Hotel California.'" I picked the distinctive opening notes, and the crowd started clapping. I sang, "On a dark desert highway…"

Deb listened and then joined me on the chorus, "Welcome to the hotel California…"

Jenny apparently texted that she was outside as we sang the third verse, Wendy scrambled to get the baby strapped back into his carrier and gathered up his bag. She mouthed, "I'll be right back."

Deb bumped shoulders with me and smiled. "Next time, give me a little notice," she whispered, before walking away.

I announced that the band was taking a brief break, and people rushed to the bar to refill their drinks. After another ten minutes, Wendy still wasn't back. I was about to go outside to see if Wendy had been kidnapped or decided to run off with my wife and kids, but just as I was getting off my stool, Wendy came bustling back in.

"I'm sorry, I'm sorry, we got talking and I forgot where I was and what I was supposed to be doing."

"No problem, we're on in a second. I could have started and caught you up."

"Jenny and I talked about our daycare situation and think we've come up with a solution. I'll fill you in on the next break. Ready to get started?"

Nodding, I wondered what plan they had concocted, but the music soon took my attention firmly away. This was what we called an easy night. Playing at Hugo's was never a difficult time. The regulars of the bar appreciated the music and never caused a commotion. Wendy could be as tame or as outrageous as she liked, and we always received positive feedback from the crowd.

Wendy and I joined Kerry and Deb's table during the break after our second set.

Deb took in Wendy's western-cut shirt and jeans. "Your tattoos are all covered. Is this a new look for you, or is this your country music persona?"

Wendy glanced down at her shirt and sighed. "I'm giving adulting a try. It seems wrong to show up at the bar toting a baby while flashing tats and flirting with the guys."

Deb smiled and nodded. "Most of us get to that point."

Curious about the conversation Wendy and Jenny had, I said, "Tell me about this solution you and Jenny have come up with for daycare."

"Peter, it's genius. I can't believe we haven't thought of it before. Jenny and I are going to hire a nanny!"

Deb nodded her approval.

"A nanny?" I asked. "We can't afford a nanny."

"Peter, splitting the cost, we can both absolutely afford a nanny. We can find someone who'll watch the little ones at our homes. Jenny and I will coordinate our schedules to decide which house the nanny will come to each day. If Jenny's leaving earlier than I am, Amy will come to our house, and if I'm earlier, Blaze will come to your house. Jeremy's old enough to let himself into the house after school, and he doesn't need a nanny. But having an adult there, he can either go home or next door if he needs help. Talk to Jenny about it, she seemed excited about the idea."

"Wait a minute," I protested. "I thought Sparky's mother was going to watch Blaze. What happened to that plan?"

Wendy's expression went from happy to glum. "She's distracted."

"She's neglecting Blaze? She can't be trusted?"

"I mentioned the boyfriend, Zeke, right?"

"Sure, she was going on a date with Zeke and that's why she wasn't available to watch Blaze tonight."

"Her dates have been spilling over into the next day. I can't rely on her to show up before I need to leave for work."

Stunned, I said, "We're talking about Sparky's mother. The one who was ready to disown Sparky and her unborn grandchild when she discovered the baby had been conceived in a fire truck."

"I think the issue was me being a harlot who'd stolen her son's virginity more than the location of the conception." Wendy paused, then added, "Please think about the nanny idea. I'd rather have my child raised by a professional who's a stranger than Sparky's bizarre mother."

Skeptical, I decided to keep my mouth shut until I talked to Jenny. Kerry gave me a look that told me I was being wise. I remembered the advice of a Marine who'd been a radio DJ before enlisting. *I've never been fired for something I didn't say.*

* * *

The next day, after I regaled Jenny with stories of our performance the night before and Jenny gushed over how precious Blaze and Amy were playing together, I broached the nanny subject.

"Wendy says you two discussed getting a nanny?"

"Peter, seriously, it's a genius idea. Why didn't I think of it earlier?"

"Funny. Wendy said the same thing."

"Sharing the wages of a nanny is such a great idea. We can find someone to do some light housekeeping and maybe even get dinner started for us each evening. I think this could free up family time after our busy days at school and work. The money we'd save from not paying for daycare and splitting the nanny cost could go into making the house more of a home for all of us, too."

"Are you sure you're okay with a stranger in our home? I've heard people say that once you let someone in, they become family. Do we want more family?"

"They also say that it takes a village to raise a child. I'm thinking the more positive influences our children have, the better."

I closed my eyes, trying to envision the future. "Fair point. I'm starting to picture a slower evening for us as a family. One where I'm able to come straight home from work without having to deal with the two kids while preparing a meal." After a moment, I reopened my eyes. "Our lives might be less stressful. I think I'm good with that picture for our family."

"Peter, I didn't even think of it that way. I don't think about how chaotic it is in the evenings for us. I mostly think of how busy mornings are, trying to get everyone dressed and in the car and ready to go. This way, Amy can sleep in if she wants to, Jeremy can have breakfast with us in peace, and we can drive together to work more often. We can work with Wendy and Sparky and their schedule. I bet baby Blaze would like to sleep in, too, not that he notices those things yet. Amy is definitely not a morning person. She'll love the extra sleep time."

Jenny smiled and replied, "I think we're in agreement. Let's get a nanny."

"Let's get together with Sparky and Wendy in the next few days and discuss particulars so we can start the search."

Jenny frowned and cocked her head. "Do you really want Sparky's input on the nanny's requirements?"

Reflecting on some of the poor choices I'd seen Sparky make, I shook my head. "Let's go with whatever you think is best."

"We need Wendy to be a part of this, too."

"Really? She's made nearly as many poor life choices as Sparky has."

Jenny conceded my point but explained, "Wendy takes her parental responsibilities seriously. Besides, they're paying half of the nanny's wages. We need her to be part of the hiring process."

I thought back to Wendy's pranks when I'd first started working. Then, about her hours of doing crossword puzzles during the workday.

"You're a thousand miles away. What's up?"

"I was just thinking about some of Wendy's shenanigans over the years."

"Like her embarrassing the minister by offering to show him the rest of the bear tattooed on her chest?"

"I hadn't even gotten to the whole tattoo thing." I snorted as a thought popped into my head. "Imagine her explaining the rainbow tattoo that disappears below her waist to a child while you're at the beach."

"I've heard rumors about the pot of gold. I suspect Wendy's bikini days are now behind her." Jenny chuckled. "Maybe she'll get one of those shorty wetsuits that cover your body from neck to mid-thigh."

I paused as I was struck by a thought. "How do you search for a nanny in Two Harbors? Do we run an ad in the paper? Is there an employment agency that screens them?"

"Those are good questions. I think Mary Gilbert was a nanny before she retired. See if she has any advice she can offer."

Chapter 7

Kathy, Mary, and Karla were excitedly chattering away at the breakfast table. While that wasn't unusual, I heard Ginny Johnson's name mentioned. Ginny, being in memory care, isn't mentioned often at the tables, and it piqued my interest.

"Hi, ladies. Gorgeous morning, isn't it?"

"Hi Peter, come join us. We had an interesting visit with Ginny yesterday and haven't been able to tell you about it until now," Kathy said excitedly.

"Tell me about it."

"You tell it, Karla, you're better at explaining these things," Mary responded.

"Okay, if you think so..."

"We do!"

"Yesterday, we were watching *Wheel of Fortune* together in the lobby. Sara was off on an errand when Becky Jorgenson came in with a man we've never seen before. We called Becky over and asked how she was doing. She responded that she was well, but that this gentleman, Perry Endicott, had gotten in touch with her over a question regarding family relationships. It seems he had done a 23andMe DNA test and discovered that his biological father was not the man he'd called Dad all these years. At 50 years old, he discovered that his mother and father weren't entirely truthful about his parentage. The 23andMe DNA test said that he and Becky were first cousins! Having grown up in Thunder Bay and never knowing about American cousins, he searched for her on Facebook. He messaged Becky and asked if she knew how they were related. Becky knew nothing about any Canadian relatives. Becky suggested he visit Ginny at Whistling Pines and take a DNA test to determine if the relationship was on Ginny's side. They were concerned as to how Ginny might respond to being asked to spit in a tube and were hoping a nurse would be available to help them out."

"I don't think Ginny is competent to consent to a DNA test," I suggested.

"Sara is Ginny's power-of-attorney, and the test was Sara's idea," Kathy explained.

"Once Sara came back, she got the evening nurse to help them out," Mary continued. "We didn't see them leave, so we're interested in what might have happened or what conversations might have taken place with Ginny."

"Peter, can you just imagine what that might be like? To call someone Dad all your life and then find out that they're not your biological father? I've known for as long as I can remember that my parents adopted me. It's never been a worry or concern, but to have had it dropped in my lap after assuming I'd been their natural-born child would have been startling for sure."

"With the advent of cheap DNA testing, I've read that a lot of fractured families have shown up." I paused and asked, "Did they get Ginny to spit into a tube?"

"Sara said Ginny did give them a sample." Mary sighed, then asked, "How bad is Ginny's dementia?"

"She's been lucid about historical things but often doesn't recognize the staff members or where her room is. Why are you asking?"

"Ginny told Sara and Perry that she had a niece who got knocked up, but she died in a car accident. Beyond that, she was emphatic that their family didn't have any Canadian relatives. Her grandparents came over from Sweden and settled in Minnesota. Ginny didn't know how Perry could possibly be a relative, especially if he was Canadian."

"I bet there's a simple answer. Maybe Perry's mother had a fling during a Duluth shopping trip."

Mary nodded. "Perry said his mother wasn't pleased about the questions he was asking. Maybe his parentage is as simple as a passing romance."

Kathy seemed deep in thought for a moment, then she asked, "Doesn't Ginny have a nephew? Maybe he got some Canadian woman pregnant while he was going to the Main U."

Karla nodded. "I suppose that's as likely as anything. I wonder if Sara asked him to spit in a tube, too?"

Kathy frowned. "If he abandoned some pregnant Canadian girlfriend, I bet he'd be reluctant to do anything to establish paternity."

Mary was deep in thought and then said, "I'm not entirely sure how that family tree stuff works. If Ginny's nephew got someone pregnant, I think that child would be Sara's second cousin, not her first cousin."

I started to walk away from the 'first/second/third cousin' discussion when a bit of information popped into my mind. "Ginny's niece was killed in a car accident? Did they mention her name?"

"Not that I heard. I assume if it had been meaningful, they would've mentioned it."

Blowing off that thought, I thanked Mary and walked back to my office. Out of curiosity, I typed 23andMe into Google. The browser took me to a story about the company's bankruptcy. Lawsuits were flying around about the security of their data and the risk of genetic diseases being revealed to the public while no one was managing their databases.

So much for digging into that aspect of the Sara/Perry story, I thought to myself.

After that, I read an article by a professional genealogist who prefaced all of her contractual arrangements with the warning, "You may discover things about your lineage you don't want to know." She added that she literally found a disconnected male parent or grandparent in ten percent of her studies. Many people, who have embraced their heritage, are deeply disturbed to find out that men in the family tree weren't the source of their DNA. I envisioned people who marched in St. Patrick's Day parades only to find out they were Polish or German. Another scenario came to mind; a family whose children didn't look alike, finding out Mom had an affair or used artificial insemination.

* * *

I walked back to the lobby and found Mary checking her mailbox. "You're just the retired nanny I was hoping to see when she wasn't surrounded by her tribe."

"What have you gotten yourself into this time, Peter?" Mary's smirk let me know she was kidding, but I was still surprised she was teasing me. I appreciated that she finally felt comfortable enough to joke with me.

"Wendy and Jenny talked this weekend about getting a nanny for Amy and Blaze." I filled her in on the conversations we'd had, and Mary's smile got bigger the more she listened. "Help me understand a nanny's role."

"I had so much fun being a nanny. Started as in-home daycare when my kids were younger, and then when the kids were adults, I answered an ad for a nanny for two children. I got the kids up, fed them breakfast, and got them off to school. After school, I made sure the kids were doing their homework, and I sometimes drove them to their after-school activities. By the time I retired, they had four children and were running me ragged. Ragged, but so happy to hang out with them. How can I help you and Jenny, Peter? I'm still retired, but hanging out with Blaze and Amy sounds like so much fun."

"I was wondering if you had any advice for us as we start searching for a nanny. Anything we should look for specifically?"

I could see the wheels turning in Mary's brain as she slowly said, "I think using your intuition and trusting your gut when you interview is the best advice I can give on your search. My last employers had several nannies before I answered their ad. They found that most applicants just didn't really understand what it took to take care of the two kids. Actually, that brings to mind something when you're interviewing. Be very clear about what kind of hours you're asking for. Do you want them to watch the kids from 6 am to 10 pm? Does your house have any quirks that the nanny should know about? Are they going to be expected to keep track of Jeremy or will you be doing that remotely? Do the children have activities you'll want the nanny to bring them to? Oh wow, I guess I do have a lot of info for you, don't I?"

"Mary, this is fantastic advice. I'm going to send Jenny to you when she has a break. I would imagine she'll want to pick your brain further."

"I'm happy to help, Peter. I know the Megchelson's appreciated my time with their kids. They ended up feeling like my own children, and when it was time to retire, I was pretty sad to not be seeing them daily anymore. Luckily, they live close by, and the kids still stop by every now and then to say hello, and I'm invited to all of their graduations and weddings. A nanny can become family. Be prepared for that."

"This is all amazing advice, Mary. I really appreciate it. Like I said, I'll talk to Jenny and let her know all you've said. I imagine she'll be tracking you down soon to ask more questions. Wendy, too. Thanks."

"Any time!"

As she walked away, it occurred to me once again that small conversations like this and asking advice of folks who'd "been there, done that" made all the difference in a person's life, whether in assisted living, a care center, or out in daily life. What a gift we have as human beings, that we can learn from each other, that no one is truly alone. I smiled at my sudden introspection as I sauntered away to find Jenny.

I'd nearly reached the nursing office when Wendy came running down the hallway toward me. "I've got a big problem," she said while trying to catch her breath.

Having been on the receiving side of several Wendy practical jokes, I was skeptical. "What's your problem this time?"

"Blaze is missing." She steered me into the nursing office, stopping in front of Jenny's desk. "I need a search party."

Looking up from a patient file, Jenny held her finger on the spot she'd stopped reading. "Who, or what, is lost?"

"Blaze!"

Jenny's superpower was being able to talk people down when they were out of control. She closed the file she'd been reading and secured it in a desk drawer. "Start from the beginning. Where was Blaze before you realized he was missing?"

"Here!"

"How did Blaze get to Whistling Pines?" I asked.

"Sparky's mother has a doctor appointment today. I suspect she caught cooties or something from her creepy boyfriend..."

I put up my hand to stop her. "TMI. I don't need to know about Sparky's mother's health."

"Anyway, I brought Blaze with me to work. He's been in his car seat or Pack 'N Play in my office the whole time."

"He disappeared while you were sitting in your office?" I asked.

Wendy glared at me. "No, I stepped out of the office to pee. He'd been asleep, so I closed the door and walked to the restroom.

When I returned, the door was open, and Blaze was missing."

"How long were you gone?" I asked.

"I don't know. How long does it take *you* to pee and wash your hands?" A thought struck Wendy, and she froze. "Pixie Kangas stopped me in the hall to ask if the new playing cards she'd ordered came in. We checked with the front desk and found her UPS delivery, then I walked back to my office. I couldn't have been gone for more than five minutes. Well, ten minutes."

"You didn't see anyone in the hallway while walking back and forth?" I asked.

Wendy sighed. "If I'd seen anyone carrying Blaze away, I would've confronted them."

"Did you see anyone walking toward your office?"

"I don't recall. I suppose I saw some people."

Jenny took out her phone and typed in a group text. "I'll have all of the aides look for Blaze."

Wendy, who is prone to hysterics over crossword puzzle clues, was melting down. "What if someone outside of the facility took him?"

"I'll call Kerry," I suggested. "However, I think we need to focus inside the facility rather than on a kidnapping."

"Let's split up with each of us taking one floor," Jenny suggested. "Peter, take the first floor and check all of the common areas. I'll knock on the second-floor residents' doors. Wendy, you take the third floor."

I punched in Kerry's cell number as I walked toward the office area. He picked up on the second ring. "What?"

"Wendy's baby is missing from her Whistling Pines office. We've started a search."

"You're serious? What was the baby doing at Whistling Pines?"

"Kerry, please set aside whatever you're doing and come here."

"I'll have the dispatcher alert the officer who's patrolling town and ask him to drive toward you. I should be there in ten minutes."

I found the KKM trio, as I'd come to call the Kathy, Karla, and Mary collective, talking near the mailboxes and explained the situation. Feeling confident they were among the more lucid and trustworthy residents; I asked them to walk around the first floor to ask if anyone had seen the baby. Howard Johnson and Lee Westfall were playing cribbage near the entrance. They assured me no one had passed them carrying a baby, and they agreed to stay there and watch for someone trying to leave with Blaze. Sherry was alone, restocking the popcorn supplies in the activity room. I enlisted her help, searching the outside perimeter and grounds.

Most times, I'm happy to engage the residents in conversations and catch up on their family events and the local rumors. A newsy conversation was the last thing on my mind while I walked from room to room, searching for Blaze. I rounded a corner and nearly bowled over Hulda Packer.

"Watch it!" she snarled, pushing her walker at me in a menacing way. "You need to talk to the kitchen. My meatloaf was so tough I had to use a steak knife to cut it up."

"I'm sorry your...meatloaf was tough. I'll ask the cooks to... (I struggled to think of any preparation technique to tenderize a hamburger blend that usually crumbles when served)...grind it up more thoroughly."

Hulda nodded, as if in agreement with my plan. "And the applesauce was excessively lumpy this morning. Have them grind that, too."

"Sure. I've got to run."

"Peter, you're brushing me off. That's inexcusable."

"Wendy's child is missing and finding him is my top priority."

"Why was Wendy's unfortunately-named child here anyway? I thought there were policies against having pets or children in the building."

"There are always children visiting their grandparents. We *encourage* that."

"That's not what I meant! We can't keep our own kids in the building."

"Right. This is a senior facility, and none of the residents should have their children living in their rooms. Now, I've got to go."

"If there aren't any children allowed, why was the school bus here yesterday?"

"The bus brought the children who sang for us yesterday afternoon. It wasn't here to pick up any children."

"Is Wendy going to have the bus pick up the child when he's old enough to attend school?"

"Listen, I have to go. Can we discuss this another time?"

"Okay, but this is my last warning about the tough meatloaf. If it's tough next time, there will be consequences."

I froze. "Consequences?" Hulda was known for her poorly considered comments and actions. "What consequences do you foresee for tough meatloaf?"

"I'm not sure, but believe me, the cooks would regret ever serving me another slice of meatloaf."

As I rushed away, I thought about that comment. *The cooks probably regret ever serving you anything!* I thought to myself as I unlocked a closet to check inside.

It's hard to say who was more startled when I turned on the closet light. Bingle had been asleep, apparently leaning against the shelving with his head down. When the light came on, he straightened up, pushing his shoulders against the upper shelf. Cleaning supplies, rags, and paper towels bounced off the back wall, then slid down the dislodged shelf. Bingle reacted to the noise and cascade of cans, bottles, and paper towels by pitching forward, causing his forehead to smash into my nose, before the two of us tumbled into the hallway.

Bingle pushed himself off of me. *"Vad tänkte du på?"*

Dazed by Bingle's head butt and smacking the back of my head against the floor, I tried to process Bingle's Swedish epithet. Running footsteps approached as my cell phone buzzed in my pocket. Not thinking clearly, I answered the phone.

"Where are you?" Kerry asked.

"I'm lying on the floor with Bingle on top of me."

"What?"

"I think he's swearing at me in Swedish."

"Why is Bingle swearing at you?"

"I interrupted his nap, and the cleaning supplies fell down."

"Did you hurt your head?"

"Just go past the activity room and take a left."

Sherry Vogel arrived and helped Bingle get onto his feet. I put out my hand for assistance getting up and she recoiled. "I think you shouldn't stand up right now."

"What?" I asked as I pushed myself up onto my elbows. The sudden change in my head's position made the room spin and I vaguely recall leaning back, then considering the pattern of the ceiling tile holes...

Luckily, or unluckily, one of the containers falling from the shelves was ammonia and that smell somehow got past the blood leaking from my nose. Like old-fashioned smelling salts, I was jarred from my delirium. Strong hands grabbed my shirt, and I was dragged away from the pooling chemicals oozing out of the closet. People started coughing and my eyes started burning.

"Bingle, hose down that chemistry experiment that's leaking out of the closet before it bursts into flames or turns into mustard gas," Kerry commanded. In the background I heard Sherry telling the dispatcher we needed an ambulance. Ripping the wrapper off a roll of paper towels, Kerry wadded up a handful of them as he guided me away from the closet. "Hold these under your nose so it doesn't look like a murder scene in the hallway."

I wiped my nose with the towels, then inspected the bright red blood. "I probably don't need an ambulance for a nosebleed."

"How many concussions have you had?"

"Counting the moose?"

"What moose?"

"I tried to chase a moose away from Dolores' house with a broom."

Kerry looked at Sherry. "Tell the dispatcher he's delusional, too."

"I'm not delusional. I almost missed the wedding because of the moose."

More footsteps approached as I closed my eyes to stop the room from spinning. "Who punched you?" Jenny asked as she took the blood-soaked paper towels from my hand.

"I turned on the lights. The next thing I remember is Bingle swearing at me about surprising him." Deeper in the facility, I heard a buzzing alarm. "Is that a fire alarm?"

Sherry and Jenny both reached for their phones as they trilled. "Someone has opened the memory care unit's emergency exit." Jenny stood and grabbed Kerry. "Please come with me in case it's one of the more *difficult* patients."

With shaking hands, Sherry tore off another bunch of paper towels and handed them to me. "I think you need some new ones." Having taken away the sodden ones, she looked at me. "You were an Army medic, right?"

"Navy corpsman but the same type of thing."

"How much blood can someone lose before they die?"

"No one has ever died of a nosebleed."

"Good. Because you look really bad right now. I mean, your skin is pasty gray, and your lips are kind of purple."

"You need to work on your bedside manner. Medical people generally try to keep the patient distracted from their injuries with encouragement and positive comments."

"I was kind of focused on not throwing up on you."

"That's a good plan," I said, realizing Sherry's background was art history and not medicine or nursing. "You're doing very well. Hang in there until Jenny comes back."

Howard Johnson and Lee Westfall rushed to us. Howard took the paper towels from Sherry. Lee took her arm and guided her down the hall.

"What happened?" Howard asked.

I explained the scenario to him, and nodded to Bingle, who was wearing what looked like a gas mask as he mopped up the spilled chemicals. "Bingle was swearing in Swedish and I rolled on the floor." I paused then asked Howard, "What does '*vad tänkte du på*' mean?"

Howard snorted. "Oh, that's a really rough Swedish curse. It translates to 'what were you thinking?'"

"Not swearing at all?"

"Hardly," Howard chuckled as Sherry led two paramedics down the hallway.

Sherry gestured to me. "I hope he doesn't die from blood loss."

The two EMTs glanced at each other. "You called us because this guy has a nosebleed?"

Sherry struggled to maintain her composure while melting down. "It was really bad. I've never seen so much blood. We've used up rolls of paper towels."

One EMT knelt next to me. His smirk said all I needed to know about my injury.

The other EMT, a young man with classic Scandinavian features led Sherry away. I wasn't sure if he was consoling her or asking her out. She blushed, then glanced at me, then directed the EMT out of sight around the corner.

"I've had a few concussions," I explained.

The EMT flashed a light in my eyes, then nodded. "I think we'll let the doctor decide whether you need further treatment."

"Is your partner married?"

The question caught my caregiver off guard. "Sven? Married?"

"It looked like he was flirting with my assistant."

A smile spread across the EMT's face as he helped me to my feet. "Sven is very single. Are you worried about your assistant?"

"Her father is a minister and she's not very experienced with worldly things."

"Well, Sven might be just the person to introduce her to the sinful opportunities that abound in Two Harbors."

* * *

I was alone in an ER exam room when Jenny and Kerry walked in. Kerry's first reaction was laughter. "I can't tell you how inappropriate it is for a professional to laugh at a patient."

"Is that you under all of those bandages and tape? I could swear it was someone trying out for a role in the next mummy movie. How many rolls of gauze did they stuff up your nose?"

"I have no idea."

Jenny whispered something to Kerry, and he left. Alone with me, she took my hand and squeezed it. "You don't have a concussion, so you can return to work once you're off the pain meds."

"Did you find Blaze?"

"We did! The memory care unit alarm went off when Ginny carried him out the emergency exit."

"Ginny Johnson had Blaze. How?"

"She was returning from having lunch with friends in the non-memory care unit when she heard him in Wendy's office. She somehow slipped away from the aide who was bringing her back to the unit, and we're still investigating how she sneaked Blaze upstairs and into the locked unit. She was convinced he was the child of the woman who was killed in the car accident at the cliff."

"The woman in the car accident was a high school student. No one said anything about her having a child, or even that she was expecting when the accident occurred."

"Right? This is how working with folks in memory care is different from independent living. You just never know what they'll say or do. Also, Wendy and I talked. We'll get together with Wendy and Sparky tomorrow night and decide how to hire a nanny. Blaze disappearing at work was the last straw for Wendy."

Chapter 8

Unable to sit quietly at home, I took two Tylenol and drove to Whistling Pines. After grabbing lunch at Culver's drive-through, I snuck in the back door to avoid the residents and sat in my office with the door closed, reading through my email and munching the last of my chicken strips. As I sat quietly in my office, savoring the silence, I glanced at an email from the Chamber of Commerce when Sherry surprised me by sticking her head into my office and asking, "Are we doing a duet for the 'No Talent' contest?"

Distracted from the Chamber of Commerce email I'd been reading, I looked up, "What contest?"

"I've scheduled the 'No Talent' contest for this afternoon." Seeing my look of confusion, she added, "We talked about this last week. I've invited the residents to sign up as performers for a talent contest. I've only got five entries, so I thought you and I could sing a duet to expand the program a bit."

Clearing my mind, I replied, "What did you have in mind?"

"You have a better perspective on what appeals to our residents. What would *you* suggest?"

"They like to hear things from their teen and young adult years. Since the average age of our residents is 80, that puts us into music from the '50s and '60s. What do your parents listen to?"

Sherry's expression told me I'd hit on a sore subject. "Being a Svenska Gotter minister, my dad listens to talk radio and Christian music."

"How about your mother?"

"She listens to whatever my dad has on."

"Let's do 'Love Potion #9.'"

"I've never heard of it. Can you find a YouTube video?"

I pulled up YouTube on my computer and typed in "Love Potion #9." I looked at Sherry, who had wrinkled her nose as we listened to the Searchers' version. "Come on, it's fun." I found The Clovers' version.

"If you sing the lead, I can handle the doo wop harmony."

Another search brought up a duet arrangement with guitar chords. I took my guitar from behind the door and quickly tuned it. I played the opening chord and sang, "I took my troubles down to Madame Rue..."

Sherry started harmonizing, "She's got a pad down on..." and then faked a deep falsetto to sing the line, "I took a drink."

When the song ended, Sherry was smiling. "It's really a stupid song, but it's kind of fun."

"Trust me, it'll be a hit."

"Print the lyrics. I'll practice them while playing the piano."

"Lieber and Stoller are the songwriters. They had a string of hits during the '50s and '60s. We could do a couple of their songs."

"Are any of them less stupid than this one?"

"Elvis Presley made 'Hound Dog' famous."

"That doesn't sound like a step forward from a love potion song. What else have you got?"

I turned to the computer and pulled up 'Poison Ivy' on YouTube. Sherry started bobbing her head as we listened to The Coasters' version. When the second chorus came around, Sherry started singing harmony to, "Poison Ivy, Poison Ivy, late at night..."

"What do you think?"

"Print the lyrics. If I sing them a couple of times, I'll remember them."

I sent the lyrics to the printer. "Really, you can read the lyrics a couple of times and remember them?"

"As long as there aren't a lot of nonsense words, I can usually remember them."

After handing Sherry the printed lyrics, I started playing the chords. She bobbed her head and sang along with me. When we got to the chorus, she set the paper aside and sang, "...late at night while you're sleeping, poison ivy comes creeping..." By the end of the song, she was swaying and singing with her eyes closed.

"That's fun. Do you think the residents will recognize it?"

"I'm sure they will."

I played the opening to "Amarillo by Morning" and sang the first bars. Sherry frowned but tapped her toe to the music. I nodded for her to sing the second verse. "They took my saddle in Houston…"

She sang harmony with me on the third verse.

When I stopped playing, she frowned. "Are you planning to sing that too?"

"No, it was a test."

"A test?"

I set the guitar aside. "You should've been a music major."

Sherry drew a breath and blew it out slowly. "I have performance anxiety. I can sing in front of the residents because I know they won't judge me. I can't sing in front of an audience who might not like me."

"You can model for an art class."

"I had my eyes closed and pretended I was sitting on a beach," she paused, then added, "I'll practice the oldies and see you in the activity room."

* * *

That afternoon, I grabbed my guitar and walked to the activity room. I was about five minutes early, but there were already thirty residents seated in groupings of three or four, dispersed around the room. The KKM trio were seated in the front row. I leaned my guitar against the corner next to the piano and approached Sherry, who had set three chairs on a riser in the front of the space.

"Who's up first?"

"Millie Peterson and Millie Pederson are going to play a 'Heart and Soul' four-hands piano duet. After that, Lee Westfall and Howard Johnson are going to stage a dramatic discussion."

"What is a dramatic discussion?"

Sherry shrugged. "Lee said it was going to be a humorous skit."

"Okay, who's up after that?"

"Mary Gilbert is going to play 'Amazing Grace.'"

Glancing at Mary, I nodded. "She's an incredible pianist. I'd bet on her being the winner."

Chuckling, Sherry nodded her agreement. "Then, Agnes and Charlotte are going to do their loon calls. After that, four women are going to sing as a barbershop quartet. Then, I have you and me as the last act."

"Loon calls?" I asked.

"I guess they're pretty good. They want to have the audience vote on who does the best one."

I heard Hulda giving someone a piece of her mind in the hallway. Karla cleared her throat to get my attention. "Peter. This is a perfect example of how sound travels faster than light.”

“I don’t think so.”

Kathy chuckled. “It’s true! We can always hear Hulda before we can see her.”

That comment brought a round of chuckles for the people seated in the room. A moment later, Hulda pushed her rattling walker into the room. She glared at me. “Peter, please fix my rattling loose wheel. Everyone hears me coming, and they stop telling all the juicy gossip.”

A titter of laughter rippled across the room, causing Hulda to give the entire room an epic stink eye.

“I’ll ask Bingle to tighten your wheels after the talent contest.”

Sherry rushed to Hulda and helped her get seated in the front row. Once Hulda was in place, she parked the walker in the back corner of the room.

As the starting time approached, the room filled with people. I gestured for Sherry to take over the Emcee duties, and I took a chair in the back corner.

The “Heart and Soul” duet got a round of applause as Lee and Howard took chairs facing each other. Once they were in place, the conversations died.

Lee glared at Howard. “So, how did you become the Whistling Pines Mayor?”

Howard puffed up. “I was appointed the mayor.”

“Who appointed you?”

Deflating slightly, "Well, I did." That comment brought a round of chuckles, mostly because everyone knew it was true.

"The job must come with great perks, right?"

"Oh yeah, the perks are great."

"Like great pay?"

"Well, not so much as I've yet to get a paycheck."

"Health insurance?"

"No, nothing to speak of. And I don't need it; Medicare does a good job for me."

"A good parking spot?"

"No need for a parking spot when I gave up driving three years ago. Besides, Peter takes me everywhere I need to go. He's a great driver." The audience tittered, and several residents turned to look at me.

"So, you take advantage of your employees, eh?" Lee was definitely on a roll.

"Now wait a minute. I would never."

"And I bet you're just waiting for the first parade this year, aren't you? You want to ride in a convertible with some hot chick at the start of the parade."

"Lee, where is this coming from? Wait. Do you want to be mayor of Whistling Pines?"

"Well, if you're willing to give it up, I wouldn't mind being in a place of authority every now and again."

"Oh ho ho, Jeri isn't letting you have the remote control to the TV anymore, is she? If you can't be the boss at home, you might as well be the boss everywhere else." The sound of feminine gasps filled the air as several residents looked at Jeri, who quickly turned pink.

"Weeeelll, I wouldn't say she doesn't let me have the remote so much as I just want to watch my shows. She won't let me watch another episode of 'Emergency.' She says that Johnny and Roy are too whiny."

"'Emergency'? I haven't watched that in ages. What channel is that on? I have to check with my kids to see if they've got me the good cable package, or if I have to get an add-on. Speaking of television, what do you think about this 'streaming television' business? I don't know if I can handle more than four channels. 3, 6, 8, and 10 were enough. When they added 21, I didn't know how I could find anything good to watch. Now we have cable and all those channels? If I were to add 'streaming,' what on earth would I get done around here? I'd be so busy watching television, I wouldn't have time to be the mayor."

"Say, Howard, since you appointed yourself mayor of Whistling Pines; how about I stage a coup d'état and take over as mayor so you can watch all that television?"

"Naw, we don't need a takeover to get you to be mayor. We can just ask your wife if she'll let you be mayor and then you can appoint yourself the new mayor."

Lee shifted to face the audience. "Jeri? May I pretty please be mayor of Whistling Pines?"

Jeri tucked a tissue in her sleeve and blushed at being the center of attention again and smiled. "Sure, Lee, as long as I get to keep the remote control when we're at home."

A round of laughter and applause ensued as Lee and Howard made their bows and took their seats.

As Lee and Howard left the stage, Mary walked over to the piano and sat down. She started playing a very simplistic version of "Amazing Grace," then went into a very stylized, almost jazz-like production of it.

After about four or five bars, Hulda called out, "What the heck is that? I don't recognize any of those notes. Can't you play the darn song like it's written?"

Undeterred, Mary continued playing as the laughter rippled through the room. She finished up the second verse and then stood and got very nice applause from the audience, aside from Hulda, who was still grumbling to herself.

Agnes and Charlotte got up to do their loon calls. Sherry introduced them and Agnes very carefully cleared her throat and made a sound that kind of sounded like a loon, which got laughter and a little bit of applause. Her partner then cleared her throat, straightened up, and went, "Here loon, here loon," which brought a big round of laughter and applause.

Sherry rushed to the podium and said, "OK, let's have the vote. Who did the best loon call?" And of course, the 'here loon, here loon' was the winner. The barbershop quartet then sang two songs and got lukewarm applause.

I pulled my guitar from the corner, walked up onto the stage to sit down next to Sherry, and started picking the lead in to "Love Potion #9." I sang the opening, which brought a round of laughter from the residents. Sherry sang harmony with the second verse and got a big laugh when she sang, "...I took a drink," in her highest falsetto.

At the end of the song, I let the laughter die down, and then I started playing "Poison Ivy." Sherry jumped in at the second bar, and about halfway through, I looked into the crowd, and I saw Wilbur Picket appearing distressed. We finished the song, receiving a nice round of applause. Sherry got up and had everyone vote on the winner of the No Talent contest, and Mary's rendition of "Amazing Grace" won as expected.

As the residents filed out, I took Wilbur aside. "You looked concerned when we sang 'Poison Ivy.'"

He drew a breath, then nodded and said, "It brought back a memory. I was one of the firemen who searched for Beth Eggleston after her car went over Lafayette Bluff. The song brought back that memory because I got one heck of a poison ivy rash that day."

Frowning, I replied, "The accident was in the spring, before poison ivy sprouted."

"That's a common myth. The stems and dead leaves still have the itchy poison on them all winter."

Satisfied that Wilbur was lucid, I asked, "You didn't find her body?"

"No. We talked about it amongst ourselves. The car was at the bottom of the cliff and had melted through the lake ice. We had no way to get down the cliff to it, and the ice wouldn't support a man's weight. We tried to push a boat over to it, but we kept breaking through and gave up. People jump from the spot once in a while, you know, to commit suicide. They're always successful. So, we figured there really wasn't any hope of finding her alive in the car."

"I suppose you checked the car after the ice melted."

Wilbur nodded. "Yeah, it was a few days later. The wind blew the ice against the bluff that year, so it mashed up that old Pinto pretty badly. There was no sign of Beth in the car." Wilbur paused, then gave me a sad look. "As terrible as it is to say this, I was relieved. She was a pretty girl, and I didn't want to find what was left of her. We assumed the shifting ice pushed and pulled her body out into the lake. You know what they say, 'Lake Superior never gives up her dead.' Well, whatever is left of her is out there somewhere."

A thought popped into mind as Wilbur spoke about Superior never giving up her dead. "The Gold Rush is playing a reunion concert at the high school. I heard they were dedicating the concert to Kenny Donaldson."

"Yeah, I'd heard that too."

"What happened to Kenny?"

Wilbur thought for a moment, then replied, "I think he was smelting. Must've tried to reach out too far and slipped, I suppose. We used to lose a couple of those drunks a year."

"I don't understand."

"The campgrounds and parking lots would get filled with drunks waiting for the smelt to start a run. They'd use long-handled nets that would reach halfway across the streams. The fish ran at night, so most of those good ol' boys would be pretty well liquored up as they lined the edges of the stream. If there was a good run, a guy could scoop up a couple dozen of them in one sweep. The problem was, if the school went up the middle or far side of the stream, those idiots would reach out too far and lose their balance. With a dozen drunks all reaching at the same time, there was jostling and shoving. Someone often got knocked in. Most often, one of the other drunks would grab him. Sometimes, he'd go ass over teakettle and his waders would fill with air, trapping the poor guy upside down." Wilbur sniffled and wiped his nose with a handkerchief. "Ain't nothing worse than motoring out into the lake to retrieve a guy who was trapped upside down with his waders full of air."

"Is that what happened to Kenny Donaldson?"

"I don't know for sure. I think it was St. Louis County who got called out for him."

"He died near Duluth?"

"Yeah, probably on the Lester River."

Chapter 9

I reflected on Wilbur's comments as the phone rang. "Peter, did you see the Chamber of Commerce email about the library program?" Madeline asked.

"I glanced at the subject and didn't open it. There's going to be a library event?"

"Yes, Meg Cochran is trying to find activities that will bring additional tourism to town. Having seen a couple of ghost-hunting television shows, I suggested that ghosts and haunted houses were big draws. I told her about my ghosts upstairs. Molly Schroeder said a ghost had been seen at the lighthouse, too."

"That's great," I replied, hoping the revelation wouldn't require my input or action.

"I got approval from the library board, and we are going to coordinate haunted tours with the historical society." Madeline paused, then added, "We heard about the séance you conducted at your house. I was wondering if you'd do the same thing here, at the conclusion of the tour?"

"Um, I didn't actually *do* the séance. One of Sherry's friends from the university was the medium."

"I heard you arranged the special effects."

Seeing my opportunity to escape from involvement evaporating, I suggested, "Sparky provided the ghostly apparition, and the tuba player from the band helped with the flickering lights."

"Perfect! Please call them. Let's sit down together and plan a similar event. How did you do the ghostly organ music?"

Unprepared to discuss my haunted music room, I froze. "I doubt the ghostly organ can be reproduced in the library."

"Okay, let's stick with the séance using ghosts and flashing lights. I've got someone at the desk. Give me a call when you've got your resources lined up."

"When is this supposed to take place?" I asked.

"It's on the C of C website, and the newspaper is running a front-page article this week. It's happening Friday night."

"This Friday?" I asked and got the dial tone. I called the library, hoping to throw cold water on the idea. After five rings, the call rolled over to the library voicemail. "Madeline, please call me back."

I walked to the activity room, hoping to find Sherry. The chairs had been stowed, and I found Bingle vacuuming. He looked up, then shut down the vacuum. "Are you looking for me?"

"I need to talk to Sherry."

Bingle frowned and scratched his head while thinking. "I think she was walking Hulda to the dining room."

The dining room was nearly full, and the servers were delivering meals to the tables. Sherry was standing in the back corner talking to Karla, Kathy, and Mary. I waved to her and stepped out.

"What's up?"

"The librarian called. They're doing a ghost tour and séance on Friday night. Madeline asked if we could supply the medium and special effects for the séance. Will you call your friend and ask if she's available?"

Sherry drew a breath, and her eyes went wide. "Dad was not pleased when he heard about the séance."

I tipped my head back. *Of course, the Svenska Gotters would be unhappy about a séance.* I thought. "If you give me Madyson's phone number, I'll call her. That'll provide you with plausible deniability."

Biting her bottom lip, Sherry stared at the front door. "No, I'll do it. Dad will be unhappy, but it's his problem, not mine."

"Are you sure? I don't want to create problems for you."

Sherry took out her cell phone. "I'll make the call. This is really short notice."

Sherry walked outside to make her call while I looked up Brian's phone number in my phone's directory. "Hi, Brian, I need a favor."

"Peter? When and where do you need me to play? Do you have an accordion player lined up, or should I call one of my friends?"

"Actually, I need your engineering expertise."

"Wow, you're desperate if you're calling me for engineering support."

"The librarian asked me to arrange a séance for Friday night. I'd like to have the lights flicker and go off and on remotely."

Brian paused so long I wondered if he'd disconnected. "Dealing with the library electrical panel might be more complicated than bypassing a fuse in the basement of your house."

"Think of it as your civic duty."

"It'd be hard to mess with the circuit breakers. Yeah, they might electrocute me or burn down the library."

"You can't make the lights flicker?"

"I didn't say that. I just can't do it through the circuit breakers. I can flip a breaker to turn the lights off. I can set up some hidden LED lights and flicker them. I'll head over to the library right now to look at their electrical panel and see where I could hide a string of LEDs."

"Perfect! Say hi to Madeline and tell her I'm working on the séance."

Sherry's smiling face told me her call had been successful. "Madyson has no social life. She thinks doing another séance would be fun. She asked if you had a particular spirit in mind. It's easier if she has a name."

I gestured for Sherry to follow me outside, and I looked up Madeline's number in my phone's directory. Pleased when she answered instead of sending me to voicemail like the last time I tried calling, I put the phone on speaker. "Hi, Madeline, Sherry has found a medium for the séance, and Brian Johnson is on his way there to talk about flickering lights."

"Wow, that's great."

I nodded for Sherry to explain the ghost identity. "My friend says she needs the ghost's name for the séance."

"Um, I don't know the ghost's name."

Laughing, I said, "I'm sure a clever librarian could research that information."

"You are so manipulative, Peter. There's nothing like throwing out a competency challenge. Hang on, there's a dusty Two Harbors history on the shelf. I'll take a look." After a pause, she came back on the line. "The first librarian was Anna Hansen. All of our ghostly events seem to happen when there's turmoil within the library and staff, so we joke that it's Anna telling us to shape up."

Sherry nodded and punched in her friend's phone number as I ended the library call. "The ghost is Anna Hansen."

Next, I punched in Sparky's number. "How are things going?" I asked.

"Peter? Are you kidding? I can't get anything done. I get calls day and night for computer support, and Blaze wakes up every time my phone rings or chirps announcing a text message."

"Put your phone on vibrate, Sparky."

"Um, oh. Sure. That's logical. It's hard to be logical at two AM when you're half awake, the kid is crying, and there's a glitch in the county computers."

"I've been there, Sparky. You're preaching to the choir."

"Oh, yeah. I forget that you've got two kids."

"I need your help."

Sparky sighed. "You aren't part of the county computer system."

"I need a ghostly apparition at the library on Friday night. A female ghost, named Anna, is going to haunt a séance."

"That would be a great diversion if I had the time…"

"Sparky, you owe me for all the things you've done and the problems you've created. This is payback."

Sighing, Sparky relented. "Fine. I need a window to display the image, and a line-of-sight location for me to set up the projector."

Paula answered the library phone when I called back. "What's across from your largest window?" I asked.

"Um, who is this, and why do you want to know what's across from our windows?"

"I'm sorry, this is Peter Rogers. I'm trying to arrange the special effects for the séance. We're going to project a ghostly image on your window, and I need to find a location for the projector."

"Wow, that's going to be awesome! Um, give me a second. The Swedish Lutheran church is across the street from our front windows. The Methbyterian Church is on the east side, but those windows aren't readily visible from the front."

"Perfect! Thank you."

"By the way, Brian Johnson is here. He said you told him to make our lights flicker."

"Yes, he's my flickering light specialist."

With a hushed voice like she was covering the phone, Paula said, "He's really enthusiastic, and a little...obsessed. He asked me what instrument I'd played in high school. He's recruiting me for the city band."

Laughing, I replied, "He doesn't take no for an answer."

"I know! I told him I haven't had my clarinet out for nearly forty years. He offered to have his wife give me refresher lessons."

* * *

Grateful to be finally home, I asked Jenny what time Wendy and Sparky were coming over. The knocking at the door and Wendy's "Yoohoo" answered my question. "Well, there goes my supper ideas, PB&J it is," I laughed as I welcomed the Plauda-Johnsons in.

"Wendy said I need to be here so we can talk about having a nanny. She said it's a glorified babysitter. I can't imagine a teenager would be interested in watching the babies during the day, don't they need to be in school?"

As I gaped at him, a giant smile broke over his face, and he laughed loudly. "Gotcha."

"Sparky, I think you've been behind a computer screen too much today."

"Ya think?"

I invited the couple in and helped Wendy get Blaze set up in the portable crib we had for Amy when she was smaller. Blaze cooed up at me as his sleepy eyes started to droop.

"Perfect," I heard Wendy over my shoulder, "He'll sleep while we talk."

As we found places in the living room, Jenny came in armed with a notepad and pen. I could see she had a number of questions already written out and was grateful she was more organized than I was for this conversation.

"Jenny, I can't say enough how excited we are that we can share a nanny for the kids. It's apparent that it's been difficult finding reliable care for him." Wendy paused to give Sparky a pained look. His mother had promised to care for Blaze prior to her boyfriend. "I can't imagine what it's been like for you two."

"Fortunately, we found a great daycare here in town when Amy was born. They'll be sad to see her go, I'm sure. I haven't had the heart to let them know we're looking for a nanny. I'll let them know once we find someone. I believe our contract would require two weeks' notice if we were leaving. I would imagine anyone working as our nanny might need to give notice where they might be working as well," Jenny mused.

"Jenny, I know you and Wendy have already talked numbers, and we're all in agreement with that, so how about how we share the nanny? Any ideas on time frames?"

Sparky brightened at my remark, "Oh, I'm so glad we don't have to talk about money. Money gives me a headache."

"I'll give you a headache," Wendy snarked.

The obvious affection the two had for each other was, in turn, sweet and surprising. Knowing how they had connected as a couple and their recent past, as well as Wendy's tendency toward snapping at Sparky, had made me wonder at times if they were working well together as a couple. Seeing their rapport was comforting.

"I have a list of questions I thought we should go through together, to decide how we want to approach this. Wendy, how about you and I look over our schedules to figure out what time frame we'd need someone, and Peter, you and Sparky talk about what you think you'd like to have the nanny do other than just watch the children?"

"That works. Sparky, let's go look at the grass out back."

"Huh? Why would I want to look at grass?"

"To get out of the room while the women talk?"

"Oh, yeah." Sparky was incredible at his IT work as well as working as a fire captain, but sometimes I wondered how much was really going on upstairs when it came to social situations.

"Do you think the new nanny would mow the lawn for you? The landlord has me mowing our lawn, and I'm..."

"Sparky, we're not asking the nanny to mow the lawn. They'll need to be able to hear the kids if they need them. Mowing the lawn might be a little noisy, right?"

"Huh, I guess you're right. I didn't think of that. Okay, what else can the nanny do besides babysitting kids?"

"I was thinking they could keep the houses tidy. I'm not an expert on keeping houses clean, but I had enough bachelor days to know how I kept my home clean. I imagine they could keep the areas clean where they spend time with Amy and Blaze at the minimum. Maybe they could start supper if we let them know what we'd need?"

"Gosh, Peter, I have no idea what to even suggest. Mom did all that stuff for me when I was living with her. She never let me touch anything in the house. She said she'd do all the inside work if I'd do the outside work."

"That explains a few things, Sparky."

Leaning close, Sparky whispered, "I never knew toilets needed cleaning. I guess Mom always did that."

"And did a new tube of toothpaste always magically show up in your medicine cabinet after you used the last of the tube?"

"Huh," was Sparky's only response. Indicating it was something he'd never considered. "Should we add that to the nanny's list?"

"No! I was being facetious." After we'd thrown a few more ideas around, we were ready to face our wives. Walking in, we saw the two huddled together over Jenny's notebook. "Well, we have a few ideas, Jenny and Wendy."

"Oh, no problem, guys, we've got it all figured out. Thanks for getting out of the house so we could figure it out in peace," Jenny smiled.

"What? I thought you wanted our input."

"You know I love you, and you know that I know that you know you have no idea what to suggest for a nanny to do other than watch children, so Wendy and I have our list all put together. Keeping Sparky busy while Wendy and I worked was perfect."

I shook my head in disbelief. Sparky seemed to be doing the same thing.

"Watching me? I'm a grown man; I don't need anyone 'watching me.'"

Wendy snorted at that and quickly tried to pull a straight face.

Jenny handed the list to me. "Do you see anything we've forgotten?"

Sparky looked over my shoulder in awe. "Wow! You guys have a whole bunch of things I'd never considered here. Like bringing the kids to the park on nice days, the library during story time, and feeding them...do you think we can find someone who knows how to make cabbage rolls? I really like cabbage rolls."

Ignoring Sparky, I asked, "We're planning to have her watch the kids at our house?"

Wendy nodded. "Well, yeah. Sparky works from home. You don't want the kids exposed to the language he uses when he's fighting with a computer."

"You're okay with us getting the advantage of the light housekeeping and not you?"

"No problem. If the kids are at your house, our house will stay tidy. As long as Sparky doesn't try to make his own lunch, that is."

"Hey!" Sparky protested. "I don't make that much of a mess."

Wendy's glare was intense. "You've never picked up after yourself in your entire life. There's no leprechaun who cleans up after you go to bed. That's all me!"

"Clean up what?"

"Empty Coke cans, potato chip bags, bread crumbs, supper dishes, your dirty clothes. Do you want me to go on?"

Sparky looked shell-shocked. "I…"

"You don't have a clue," Wendy snapped. "It's time for you to take a class in adulting."

"I have responsibilities at the firehouse. I don't have time to pick up stuff around the house."

Jenny stepped in. "I don't want to get into the middle of your lifestyle issues here, but it sounds like you two need to talk through some things at home."

Sparky's pleading look toward me was pathetic. "I don't want to go home right now."

I patted his shoulder. "Even Jeremy clears the table and picks up his own clothes, buddy. We're working on him doing his own laundry."

Sparky glanced at Jeremy, who nodded. Then he hung his head. "I s'pose I can do more around the house." He perked up. "Unless we could find a nanny who…"

In unison, Wendy and Jenny said, "NO!"

Chapter 10

After checking emails, I grabbed my mug and walked to the dining room. Breakfast was in full swing, and the dining room was filled with the sound of clinking silverware and dozens of discussions. After drawing a cup of coffee, I turned and studied the crowd. No one seemed stressed or unhappy. Feeling confident I didn't need to head off any arguments or problems, I turned to leave.

Jeri's dainty "Achoo!" caught my attention. She and Lee were sitting at a table with Dottie and Alma. When I smiled at Lee, I realized something about him was different. It took a few minutes to reach them, walking through the arrayed tables and saying hello to all of the smiling faces.

As I pulled a chair over from another table, Jeri sneezed again. "Bless you," I said.

"This crazy sneezing has to stop," Jeri said, sniffling.

"I'm surprised she hasn't faded away to nothing with the tiny bit she eats between sneezes," Alma offered while Dottie was suddenly focused on finding the raisins in her oatmeal.

I stared at Lee for a moment before I realized how he'd changed. "Lee, you've always been bald on top. When did you decide to shave your entire head?"

Lee paused to consider his answer. "Well, I didn't shave it."

"Your head wasn't bare yesterday," I observed.

"I decided to do whatever I could to help Jeri overcome her sneezing spells."

"You didn't use Nair?"

He nodded.

I stifled a laugh by sipping coffee. "It appears the Nair treatment didn't solve the problem."

Jeri sneezed again and shook her head. "Not at all. And our sink is clogged with all the hair that came off."

I looked at Lee's head. "You didn't have that much hair..." I stopped. "You didn't?"

Lee rolled up one sleeve, exposing a hairy arm. "I figured that flu bug was like a head cold."

Hulda had been eavesdropping from the next table over. "The Nair treatment isn't effective unless all of his hair is gone."

I looked at Lee, who shook his shiny head. "No way. I only did my scalp."

Jeri sniffled and sneezed again. "I told him that stupid apiary flu wasn't the problem. I just don't know what could be causing this. I don't sneeze all night or when we're watching television."

"When do you sneeze the most?"

"Achoo! My nose starts running every time we come down for a meal. I wonder if I'm allergic to something we're eating?"

"Talk to Jenny. I think she could suggest an over-the-counter antihistamine for you to take before meals."

Mary waved from a nearby table and pulled out the fourth chair at their table. "How is your nanny search going?"

"The ad will appear in the newspaper tomorrow. First, I wonder if anyone will respond. Then I'm anxious about who might respond. I'd love to have someone like one of you three to show up for an interview. I'm scared that some tattooed biker dude will ride up on his Harley."

"Things have a way of working out, Peter. Trust your instincts."

The twinkle in Kathy's eyes prefaced her comment. "Maybe Hulda would like to come and live with you as a nanny. I could suggest it."

Karla broke out laughing, and Mary covered her mouth to not spit her mouthful of coffee on us. "That's not even funny."

Karla put her hand on my arm. "It's hilarious! Good one, Kathy."

They were still laughing when I left. I was halfway to my office when Sherry called my name from behind. "I heard you were looking for a nanny."

"It hasn't been advertised yet. How did you hear about that?"

"I overheard Jenny and Wendy talking about how they were going to interview people."

"There's going to be an ad in tomorrow's newspaper."

"Would you interview an art history major?"

"Are you thinking about a career change?"

"Not me, Madyson graduated and isn't getting any interviews. Her apartment lease runs out at the end of the month, and she's trying to come up with an option besides moving back to her family farm. She's from a big family, and she might really enjoy watching three kids."

"Mention her to Jenny. I don't know of any reason we'd exclude her from consideration unless she's got a criminal record."

Frown lines furrowed Sherry's forehead. "Oh, would her past drug abuse be a problem?"

"Um, yeah."

Sherry burst into a smile. "You are so gullible. No wonder Kathy, Mary, and Karla have so much fun pulling your leg."

"Yeah, I'm missing the sarcasm gene."

Bingle joined us in the hallway outside the dining room. Looking smug, he said, "Hulda won't be sneaking up on anyone."

"What?" Sherry asked, having missed the conversation after Bingle's Swedish epithet.

Smirking, Bingle replied, "I put a drop of salt water on one of Hulda's walker wheels when I tightened them. It squeaks every time it turns. The best part is, she can't hear the high-pitched squeak, so she doesn't know she's like a cat with a bell on its neck."

The breakfast crowd was departing, and we all turned toward the door as a slow-paced squeaking sound came from the dining room. A moment later, Hulda walked out with three of her friends. A high-pitched squeak accompanied every rotation of the walker's wheels. Seeing Sherry, Bingle, and me smiling at her, she demanded, "What are you staring at?"

"I just commented to Bingle and Sherry about how perky you seemed today."

Unsure of my sincerity, Hulda frowned. "Don't you have some Commission of Competence meeting to attend, or something?"

"No, the Chamber of Commerce isn't meeting today."

As Hulda shuffled away, Sherry bumped elbows with Bingle. "That is better than a bell on a cat. Good job."

* * *

Back in my office, I checked the newspaper's website for the nanny ad. I read it several times, trying to picture who would respond.

Wanted: a nanny to watch an infant, toddler, and middle school child. Must have a valid driver's license. Experience and references preferred. Live-in available. Salary negotiable. Jenny's phone number followed.

I heard footsteps approaching a moment before Brian stepped into my office and sat in the guest chair. "I heard you are looking for a nanny."

"Where did you hear that?"

He pointed at my computer screen. "It's online."

"Please tell me you're not here to apply for the job."

Brian snorted. "I'm not nanny material. Young children don't react well to tuba music."

"Not only small children," I said in a theatrical aside.

"Hey!" Brian laughed. "I'm sitting right here."

"No tuba joke today?"

Brian leaned back and thought. "What's the difference between a tuba and an onion? No one cries when you slice up a tuba."

"I think that might be over Jeremy's head."

"How about a nanny joke? When you're a kid, your parents tell you what time you have to be home. When you have children, the nanny tells you what time you have to be home."

"I like that one."

As I wrote the joke on my notepad, Brian asked, "Would you consider a clarinet player for a nanny job?"

I shrugged. "What's the punchline?"

"There's no punchline. Ellie Ogren, our second-chair clarinetist, is a seasonal employee at Gooseberry Falls State Park. She's looking for a steady job."

"Sure, have her call Jenny."

Brian stood, then paused at the door. "Speaking of nannies, you know who used to be the Megchelson's nanny, right?"

"Why is that name familiar to me?"

"Bobby Megchelson's band is playing at the high school."

Still confused, I shrugged.

"Bobby Megchelson changed his name to Cliff Silver when The Gold Rush became famous."

In a flash, the dots connected in my head. "Oh, I remember now...and Mary Gilbert told me she'd been Megchelson's nanny!"

Brian nodded. "She was the nanny for Bobby's cousins. She taught Bobby how to play the piano. That's where his music interest began."

"Wow, this really is a small town."

* * *

The dining room was empty when I returned, so I walked to Mary's room and knocked on the door. After being invited in,

I sat in a rocking chair across from her recliner, where she'd set a book aside. "What's up?" she asked.

"You were Megchelsons' nanny."

After a moment of hesitation, she nodded. "I was."

"You taught their nephew, Bobby, to play the piano."

Mary smiled as she reflected on the past. "He was the most musically gifted student I've ever had. After a few weeks of lessons, he was composing his own songs."

"You've never mentioned that."

"What is there to say? It was one of the most rewarding parts of my life. I got to open a door for a musician who surpassed my abilities. That's really the most any teacher can hope for."

"Have you spoken to Bobby?"

Mary chuckled. "Once Bobby took his stage name, he left Two Harbors behind him. I don't think he's been back to Two Harbors in forty years, and I doubt that he's thought of me since he left."

"Does he have relatives in town?"

"All of the other Megchelson children went to college and moved away after graduation. I get Christmas cards from the two girls. I haven't heard from the boys in decades."

"Are any of the other children talented musicians?"

"They all played the piano. They could hit all of the right keys in the correct order.

They would study the music as they played, stopping to turn the pages.”

“What about Bobby?”

“He’d play a piece through once or twice, then he’d have it memorized. When he played…”

“He became one with his instrument.”

Mary smiled. “As you do.”

“Are you going to the concert?”

Mary paused, then shook her head. “Rock is really not my genre. I’m more into traditional church music.”

“Your rendition of ‘Amazing Grace’ was inspiring.”

“Thank you. But it was still ‘Amazing Grace’, not ‘Love Potion #9.’”

I nodded to the keyboard sitting to the side of the living room window. “Will you play something for me?”

As she moved from her recliner to the piano bench, she asked, “Did you have something special in mind?”

“Play ‘Stairway to Heaven.’”

After a moment of silence, she reached out and started playing the song’s introduction. “There’s a woman who’s sure all that glitters is gold…” She stopped singing and playing after the first verse.

“You could play for Wendy’s band.”

Mary smiled. “I appreciate the compliment. However, the bar scene isn’t my thing. I feel more fulfilled playing hymns in a church.” She returned to her recliner and picked up her book. "Was there something more?"

"What should I know about Cliff Silver?"

"Nannies don't share stories. We're part of the family, and we don't air dirty laundry."

"That's reassuring to know as we start our nanny search," I said as I stood.

"I can't imagine you and Jenny have dirty laundry to air."

"I'd like to believe that. On the other hand, we're planning to share the nanny with Wendy and Sparky."

Mary blew out a breath. "Wow. That's right. Wendy is a bit more...prone to drama than you and Jenny. You might want to ask your nanny to sign a non-disclosure agreement."

I paused with my hand on the doorknob. "Did you know the reunion concert is dedicated to Kenny Donaldson?"

A pained smile flickered on Mary's face. "I suppose that's fitting."

"What do you remember about Kenny?"

"He was also one of my students. Bobby was more talented. Kenny was studious and had to practice."

"I heard he was the original keyboardist for The Gold Rush."

"Performing with the band wasn't as difficult as playing an etude. Most of the time, he just played chords."

"Do you know what happened to Kenny?"

"He...um...did one of the stupid high school boy things. They went smelting in Duluth. Kenny slipped and fell in..."

"You said, 'they' went smelting. Who was with him?"

"I assume it was their usual group. The guys in the band were always together." Mary paused, then added, "I was the organist at Kenny's funeral."

Chapter 11

Madeline looked up from the computer and was surprised to see the police chief and me walk in. "Is something wrong?"

"I have a piece of information I've been withholding from you, and we need your help," I replied.

"I suppose you don't have to tell me all your secrets, Peter. What's the information, and how can I help?"

"The tape in the dusty drawer was a demo made by someone in The Gold Rush. It was an early version of the band's hit song," I explained.

"That's interesting. I found a little brass plaque that says the table was donated by the Megchelson family. Does that mean anything to you?"

I smiled. "Bobby Megchelson took the stage name Cliff Silver. I'd wager the table belonged to Cliff's parents or grandparents."

"Sure!" Madeline replied, "Maybe it was in their house when he was in high school and he hid the tape there. When the band got famous, he was on the road and moved to Las Vegas. I guess his grandparents died and his family donated the table to the library, not knowing there was anything of value in the drawer."

Kerry nodded his agreement. "Cliff Silver had Bingle break into the drawer. I wasn't planning to do anything about that unless you felt he should be cited for vandalizing the drawer."

"Bingle already repaired the drawer, and it now has a functioning lock. I don't need you to do anything more." Hesitating, Madeline asked, "What help did you need?"

"My Whistling Pines residents recalled a car crash back in the 1970s where a girl was apparently killed. I did an internet search and came up empty. I hope you have old newspapers that might have a story about the accident."

Madeline nodded toward a hallway behind the desk. "All of the newspapers are back here, with yearbooks and other local interest materials." She unlocked the door and flipped a light switch. "The newspapers are down here, to the left."

Kerry followed and watched as the librarian pulled out a huge folder marked 1971. "I thought they'd be on a CD or microfilm."

"I suppose digitizing them has never been a budget priority. We have the actual printed copies. Do you know what year?"

"I just heard '70s. It was probably a big enough story to make the front page."

"Let's each flip through a year. If we're only looking at the headlines, we should be able to get through that entire decade in a few minutes." Madeline paused, then said,

"If you're busy, I can do this and call when I find an article."

Kerry chuckled as he started flipping through 1972. "As sad as this sounds, I'd rather be here looking at old newspapers with you than I would be at my desk dealing with paperwork and irate people."

"Ah, this is an escape."

Kerry nodded. "I'd call it a respite."

We were more than halfway through the '70s when Madeline reached out and touched Kerry's shoulder. "Chief, I think I've found it." She turned the newspaper so Kerry could see the headline. "Local Girl Missing After Car Crash." They stood side by side and read the front-page article from April 23, 1976.

Halfway through, Kerry pulled out a pen and a notepad. "I'm not familiar with this location. Where is this Lafayette Bluff referenced as the location of the crash?"

"I've got a Lake County map on the wall."

Quickly scanning the location names, Madeline stopped with her finger on a spot a few miles north of the city. "The cliffs here are called the Lafayette Bluff. I think this is about where the tunnel is located."

"When was the tunnel built?"

"I just had a sixth grader ask that. He was writing an essay about this, the first 'hard rock' tunnel built in Minnesota." Madeline pulled out another newspaper, which showed the process of drilling and blasting the tunnel, including an aerial photograph showing old Highway 61, where it ran along the top of the cliff prior to the opening of the tunnel.

"Wow!" Kerry said. "The highway ran right along the top of the cliff. It doesn't look like there's even a guardrail protecting it."

"I suppose that's how the crash occurred," Madeline opined. "The girl was driving along the top and got distracted or lost control of her car. What a terrible tragedy."

Kerry nodded. "The article says her car burst into flames. By the time rescue teams got to the cliff, the car had melted through the ice. Divers recovered her car after the lake ice melted, but they never located her body."

"Tragic." Madeline turned away from the map. "Is there anything else I can help you with, Chief?"

Kerry glanced at his notes. "If I think of anything else, Peter or I will give you a call."

Madeline walked us to the front door and said, "Thanks for stopping by. Working with you and Peter on mysteries is more interesting than most anything else I do."

"Really? We're more interesting than collecting fines for overdue books?"

Madeline leaned close and whispered, "Don't tell anyone, I don't usually enforce those fines. Just the threat of a fine is enough to get most people to return their books on time. Besides, you'd be amazed at how many people are downloading books through our database. That's even better because the book is taken off their reader on the expiration date. No fines required."

* * *

Kerry and I drove out of town on Highway 61 until he approached the tunnel. Taking the last turnoff before entering the tunnel, he drove down the narrow road. "It's hard to believe this was once the main thoroughfare between Minneapolis and Thunder Bay. There must've been dozens of head-on accidents and people running off the road, back then."

"I suppose it was considered scenic. Only a cop would be more concerned about the dangers than this spectacular view."

Stopping at the point closest to the cliff, Kerry switched on his light bar and donned a fluorescent yellow vest. We walked along the shoulder of the road, now protected by a guardrail. Looking almost straight down, I said, "It would've been difficult to lower a rescue crew down to the lake. I suppose there was ice, so they couldn't access this spot by boat."

Looking back along the car's likely path to the cliff, Kerry asked, "I wonder how well they searched this area? There are ledges, nooks, and crannies where a body could've been thrown clear of the car."

A pickup slowed as it passed his squad, then it stopped next to him. The young driver rolled down his window and asked, "Is everything okay?"

Kerry waved and nodded, "Yeah, but thanks for stopping and asking. I appreciate it."

The guy drove off, leaving Kerry looking up and down the road. "I wonder how long it was before someone noticed that a car had gone over the cliff? There aren't any trees. Unless someone noticed skid marks, who would've known the car had gone over the cliff? I wonder if the crews only searched where the car went over the cliff, and she hit something and was thrown out of the car before it went over? I wonder if there's a police report in the files?"

When he ended his string of rhetorical questions, I said, "Take me back to work while you try to answer those questions."

Kerry was silent as we drove back to town. Instead of driving to Whistling Pines, he parked outside the police station.

"You missed my turn."

"I thought you'd want to be part of the solution."

I struggled to keep up with his determined stride. "I'd prefer to let you do that police stuff and be happy with a phone update."

* * *

At the Two Harbors Police Station, Kerry had to ask the part-time department clerk where he could find a file from 1976. She stared at him for so long without answering, I began to wonder if she'd heard the question. "There are boxes of files in the basement. I suppose it might be down there."

"Do I have the key to open the storage room?"

"Huh? Good question, Chief. No one has been in there since I started in 2002. If you don't have a key, there's a keyring in the file cabinet marked 'misc.'"

"Why don't you save me a trip up and down the stairs and give me the 'misc.' keyring now?"

After examining the lock, Kerry quickly flipped through the thirty or more keys on the 'misc.' ring, eliminating most of the keys and trying the probable ones in the lock.

"Are you wondering what all of these other keys open?" I asked.

Kerry paused and looked at me. "Not really."

"Maybe this room is filled with lockers or boxes secured with padlocks. Or maybe the store owners gave the police keys so they could get in during an emergency."

Kerry ignored me and kept searching for the key to open the storage room. About halfway around the ring, he inserted the correct key, and the latch released. The basement room was unlit and smelled of mildew. He shone his flashlight while I looked for the light switch. Once the room was lit, we looked at three rows of shelving, each twenty or more feet long and all reaching from the floor to the ceiling.

Kerry blew out a breath. "Let's turn off the lights, lock the door, and throw away the key." He dismissed that thought, and we worked our way down the nearest shelves. I was pleasantly surprised to find the boxes clearly labelled with the dates of the contents, all arranged chronologically. On the second set of shelves, Kerry located the box marked April-June 1976.

He set the box on a table and flipped through the contents, which included everything from crime scene evidence to case files. He pulled the file marked April. "This must be it."

I turned off the lights and he relocked the door. At his desk, we flipped through the contents, which included everything from traffic citations to reports of family abuse and two bar fights.

I found a neatly printed label on a manila folder that read *Lafayette Bluff Car Accident*. "I've got it."

The handwritten notes were faded, and the paper was yellowed. Kerry set aside the half dozen black and white photos that fell from the folder. Struggling to decipher the handwriting, we waded through the report, taking turns guessing the faded words.

The accident was reported by a truck driver delivering Duluth newspapers to the North Shore communities. He'd noted a fire below the cliff and pulled over to investigate. Seeing the burning car on the ice, he called the police department from a pay phone in Beaver Bay, then continued with his delivery route.

The State Patrol was on the scene when the Two Harbors Police arrived. Together, we determined that the fire, which had mostly died out, involved a car that had skidded off the cliff.

Kerry straightened up and stretched his back. "There is no mention of calling out firemen, apparently because the responding officers felt the crash wasn't survivable. After sunrise, the fire chief and two firemen arrived at the scene. The car had landed on frozen Lake Superior, and the fire apparently melted the ice sufficiently to allow the metal wreckage to break through."

The report went on, "Harlan Orenson, a local rock climber, was contacted, and he rappelled down the cliff. He found evidence of the car striking multiple rock outcroppings on the way down, but he didn't find the driver, nor was he able to read the car's license plate. He guessed the car's twisted and burned metal had been a Ford Pinto. The driver's door was open, and Harlan thought the driver might've jumped out or been ejected from the vehicle before the car went over the cliff."

Kerry flipped to the last pages and found a note that the license number had been found and the owner, Elizabeth Eggleston, was missing from her parents' house. The search for her remains had been suspended after two days.

The final page of the report was handwritten by the investigating officer in faded blue ink. After interviewing Elizabeth's friends without developing any leads, Tammi Mitchell told me Beth had broken up with her long-time boyfriend and partied with 'half of the hockey team.' Her tone made me think Elizabeth had been bullied and ostracized. No one, including the missing girl's family, identified any current romantic relationship.

Kerry arranged the pictures on his desktop and said, "There's really not much to see. The weeds are knocked down where the car's tires rolled through, but there's nothing to indicate this was anything but an accident." He drew a deep breath and went back to the handwritten notes. "The driver was Elizabeth Eggleston, and her body was never recovered."

"Beth."

"What?"

"The song I found was written to Beth. You need to talk to Cliff Silver. I'll wager a burger that he knew Beth and had knowledge of the accident."

Kerry gathered the file spread on his desk. "His name isn't mentioned anywhere in the report. I'm busy with some filing. Find Cliff. See what he remembers about Elizabeth."

Ignoring Kerry's suggestion, I asked, "The report would have said Robert or Bobby Megchelsen, not Cliff Silver – it's a stage name, remember? And also, you're discounting this Tammi Mitchell's comments?"

"She didn't know anything. She just wanted to dish dirt on the Eggleston girl. Today, we would call it bullying. Why don't you want to find this Cliff Silver character and talk to him?"

"Because I'm not a cop."

"You're incognito."

"Kerry, I'm employed by Whistling Pines. I'm not your personal investigator."

"Your boss appointed you the police liaison. You've been helpful."

I sighed. "When did I agree to be your personal slave? Is there an endpoint to this obligation?"

"How long did it take Moses to lead the Israelites out of slavery?"

"Kerry, they wandered in the desert for forty years."

"Let's have this discussion again in thirty-nine years."

* * *

I was staring at the phone, trying to determine how to find Cliff Silver, when Sherry peeked into my office. "Do you have a second?"

I nodded toward my guest chair. "I'll give you a second if you help me with a problem. How would you search for someone who's visiting town?"

"If it's someone here on vacation, I'd call the resorts. If it's someone here to visit their mother at Whistling Pines, I'd call the Two Harbors Motel. Otherwise, I'd call their relatives. Maybe they're staying at someone's house."

"Great suggestions, thanks. What can I do for you?"

"You've had me sing harmony with you a few times. Once you sing it for me, I can repeat it, but I don't really understand why it works."

"How much theory do you want? If you want depth, I suggest you register for a music class. They'll teach you chord theory and diatonics. If you just want an overview, I can explain a few basics."

"Start me with a few basics."

I took out my guitar and strummed a chord, then plucked each of the strings individually. I explained the steps in a three-note chord.

"In 'Poison Ivy' I was singing the second note of the chord, right?"

"A lot of the music from the '50s to the '70s uses a third down harmony. I think The Everly Brothers did it about the best of anyone."

"I don't think I've ever heard of them."

I pulled up the chords and words on my computer, then played the opening to "All I Have To Do Is Dream." I sang the first verse. "Sing along with me like you've been doing, a third higher."

We were harmonizing on "...anytime, night or day. Only trouble is, gee whiz..." When Jenny stepped into my office wearing a huge grin, I stopped and asked, "Is there something funny?"

"Not at all. I was just enjoying the music. The timbre of your voices mesh so well, it gives me chills."

Sherry nodded. "I've sung in the school choir and with a couple of garage bands. Sometimes two voices together are like fingernails on a chalkboard. When we're harmonizing together, I sound like Peter singing an alto falsetto harmony with his tenor melody."

Jenny nodded toward my desk. "Harmonize on the song from the scrap of paper Bingle found in the library."

I took out the copy I'd made and strummed the chords, then I handed it to Sherry. "Sing the melody."

Sherry sang the melody, and I joined in with a third lower harmony. Nancy, the director, stepped through the door behind Jenny. "That's lovely, but it's the wrong name."

I stopped playing and stared at her. "The wrong name?"

"That's the song 'Barb.' I've heard it a hundred times. Sing the whole song."

"All I have is the chorus."

I set the guitar back into the corner. "Please excuse me, but I need to locate Cliff Silver." The three women left me to Kerry's assignment.

Before I could act on that thought, my cell phone buzzed. "This is Peter."

"Are you the person who advertised for a nanny?"

Knowing my phone number wasn't in the nanny ad, and unprepared for a discussion, I stammered, "My wife's phone number is in the newspaper ad. How did you get my number?"

"Brian Johnson mentioned you during the band rehearsal. I'm one of the flute players." The girl paused, then asked, "You are looking for a nanny, right?"

"Um, yes. We're looking for a nanny."

"I've never been a nanny, but I have a lot of babysitting experience. Would that be okay?"

Thinking the person sounded more like a teen than a nanny-aged applicant, I asked, "Do you live in Two Harbors?"

"Yes, I'm a senior at the high school."

"We're actually looking for someone who could get my son off to school in the morning and watch the two younger children during the day. I'm afraid your classes would conflict."

"I could drop out."

"Um, no. That would be a bad solution. Thanks for your interest."

Almost as an afterthought, I looked up numbers for the Two Harbors motels. I found Cliff Silver on my second try. "I'd like to leave him a message."

"I just saw him walk through the lobby a few minutes ago. I'll connect you with his room."

I didn't have a script prepared for a Cliff Silver interview and tried to organize my thoughts while the phone rang. A woman answered, and I said, "I'm sorry. I was looking for Cliff Silver."

"Hang on. He's right here."

"This is Cliff."

"Mr. Silver, I'm Peter Rogers...with the Two Harbors Police. Do you have a moment?"

Curious, Silver replied, "What's this about?"

"Elizabeth Eggleston disappeared when her car went over Lafayette Bluff. Do you remember that?"

"Whew! That's ancient history."

"Tell me what you remember about the days before her disappearance."

Cliff chuckled, "There's a lot of alcohol, some drugs, and a lot of gigs since high school. I don't remember anything about a specific time or day anymore."

"She'd broken up with her boyfriend after the prom and was at loose ends. We heard she'd been partying in the weeks before she disappeared."

"As I recall, Beth wasn't really a party girl."

"One of the girls interviewed after the car accident told the police Beth had been partying with the hockey team."

"You do understand that's a way of saying she was sleeping around. That wasn't Beth's style."

"The way you're talking about her makes me think you knew her better than you're letting on."

"Beth was dating our keyboardist."

"Kenny Donaldson? I heard you're dedicating your concert to Kenny."

"Yeah, well, he was with us at the beginning."

"What happened to Kenny?"

I heard a woman's voice in the background, then Silver said, "My wife says we need to make a trip to Duluth for batteries. I've got to run."

"One quick question."

"I've really got to go." Then he hung up.

Leaning back in my chair, I studied the ceiling and reran the conversation. Cliff obviously knew Beth well but was reluctant to admit it. He wasn't forthcoming about the relationship between Beth and Kenny. When questioned about events immediately before her disappearance, he hung up. Beth wasn't "sleeping with the hockey team," she was dating the band's keyboard player.

Unsure of what to do with the information, I called Kerry and told him about the interview.

"He answered your questions?"

"Yes, he seemed okay with it."

"Did you tell him you were a fellow guitar player or something?"

"I might've mentioned I was with the Two Harbors Police."

Kerry sighed. "And he was willing to accept that over the phone?"

"Yes."

"In my experience, celebrities are very distrustful of people claiming to be cops or reporters. They usually want to see a badge or want to call their lawyer before answering questions."

"Back up. I got him to answer a few questions. He knew Beth better than he wanted to admit. He assured me she wasn't a party girl and had been dating Kenny Donaldson. When I asked if anything had happened in the days before Beth's disappearance, his wife interrupted, and he had to leave."

"Hmm, I wonder if Cliff's wife knows what happened to Beth, and she doesn't want Cliff blabbing about it?"

"If you'd done something significant enough to cause your bandmate's ex-girlfriend to kill herself, would you tell Deb about it?"

Kerry snorted, "That's not an issue. Is that topic something that's come up with you and Jenny?"

"No. I'm just speculating on why the woman with Cliff would interrupt his call."

"Sometimes the obvious answer is the correct one."

"They needed to drive to Duluth to buy batteries? There are batteries at the corner convenience store. She was trying to end the call."

"Again, maybe the obvious answer is the correct answer. Maybe she just felt he'd said enough to a cop, and she wanted him to stop talking about things from his old life." Kerry paused, then added, "Speaking of ending calls. I need a fresh cup of coffee. Call me again when you have anything concrete to share."

Chapter 12

Frustrated by both calls, I decided to walk around while I thought about it. I was walking past Dottie Preston's apartment when I heard a strange sound like a dying goose. Knowing that anything can happen at Whistling Pines, I decided to try the door to see if Dottie was all right. Opening the door, I was shocked to see a cat run out and into the hallway. Not as surprised as Bingle, though, when the cat ran right up his leg and into his arms.

"Peter! Cat? Why does he like me?" Bingle whisper-shouted.

"I opened Dottie's door, and it ran out."

"We don't allow pets for the residents, do we? That's a lot of extra cleaning in the hallways if we're going to have all that fur and dander. Aren't allergies a problem for many people? Is Nancy letting this happen? I thought after Axel's dog, we banned pets."

In shock for a moment as I had no idea Bingle had that much information stored in his head; it took me a few seconds to register what he had said. "Bingle, we've not gone back on that rule, and you're right, it is a huge allergy problem. Dottie must have hidden him in her apartment. I'll find her and see what's going on."

"What about the cat, Peter?"

"Can you lock him in a maintenance closet for now? Once I talk to Dottie, we'll see where the cat can go."

"Peter, how can I hide him?"

"Can't you put him in your coat and go down the back stairs? Residents don't use that stairwell as often."

"I'll try."

Smiling to myself in disbelief, I went down the main stairs in search of Dottie. On my way down, I was met by Jenny, who looked like she was on a mission. I hated interrupting her mission, but I also knew she would want to weigh in on this discussion.

"Jenny, I think I found the cause of the 'apiary flu.'"

"Peter, you're ridiculous, you know there's no such thing."

"I know that, but you're not gonna believe what just happened." As I quickly and quietly filled her in on the cat situation, the look on her face grew from shocked to incredulous to amazed.

"How on earth did she have a cat in her apartment all this time and we never knew?"

"I have no idea. I'm going to talk to Dottie right now. Do you want to join me?"

"I would, but I'm taking meds to Lyndon Hjelmborg. I'll find you if I'm able once I'm done."

I continued down the stairs and didn't run into anyone else who might be able to help with the conversation. I briefly considered talking to Nancy first, but decided I'd rather have the whole story from Dottie before I went to Nancy with it.

Finding Dottie in the great room with a few residents, I asked if she would join me outside on the patio for a quick breath of fresh air.

Puzzled, she followed me, but as soon as the door was closed, she asked what was going on.

"I was walking past your apartment and heard a strange sound, Dottie. I was worried about you being hurt, so I opened the door, and a cat ran out. Any idea how a cat got into your apartment?"

Her face went white when I mentioned the cat, so I knew she was hiding something. "I don't know what you're talking about" was definitely not the answer I was expecting from Dottie. She was a straight shooter, so lying wasn't her usual M.O.

"Dottie, you honestly have no idea how a cat got into your apartment?"

Spluttering a bit, she finally confessed that yes, she did have a cat in her apartment and that she, "was so lonely at night, I thought the cat might be good company."

"How long have you had the cat, Dottie?"

"About four months. My daughter's best friend had it and couldn't keep it anymore, so I volunteered to take him. He'd been toilet-trained, so I didn't have to have a litter box for him. I knew that would keep the smell down in my apartment. I know that pets aren't allowed in the building, but I thought if I kept him locked up in the bathroom when I wasn't in my apartment, no one would ever know. I must have forgotten to shut the bathroom door when I left this morning."

"Dottie, you know I have to let Nancy know about this, right? Pets are prohibited due to the possibility of residents' allergies. This could be why Jeri has been so miserable lately."

"I didn't even think about allergies. Jeri is my friend. The idea that I am the reason why she's been feeling ill lately makes me feel bad. I suppose I'll call my daughter and see if she can come and take him."

"That would be a good idea, Dottie. I'll still have to let Nancy know about it. I don't know if she'll need any additional information from you, but don't be surprised if she comes to visit. There may have to be some deep cleaning done in your apartment to remove the cat hair. Nancy will let you know if that's the case."

After letting her know that Bingle had put the cat in the storage room, Dottie and I went back inside. She went to her apartment to call her daughter, while I went to talk to Nancy.

* * *

"I feel like the situation with Dottie is resolved, but as administrator, I imagine

173

there will be procedures you'll have to follow, right?"

"Peter, this is just so amazing. I can't believe that for four months we've had a cat in the building and just now are finding out. People will do just about anything to have a pet now, won't they? I've even heard of dogs using litter boxes now!"

"Nancy, there's no way a dog will use a litter box."

"Oh yes, they will. My Iowa cousin got a Shih-tzu from a breeder seven years ago that had been trained to use the litter box as a puppy. The breeder had Shih-tzus and Labradoodles that were all litter box-trained by the puppy's mothers. She said it was great because she didn't have to worry about taking the puppy out in the middle of the night to pee. Truck drivers were scooping the breeder's dogs up by the armload. Saved them hours and money by having a dog use a litter box instead of having to stop every two hours for the dog to do its business."

"Seven years of cleaning up a dog litter box? That has to be a job."

"You'd think, right? But her dog decided at about a year old that he was a 'big boy' and would do his business outside instead."

"Do you think we need to check all the apartments for pets? Maybe someone else has met this dog breeder in Iowa and has brought a puppy home now, too?"

"Peter, I wouldn't put it past some of our residents but no, we don't need to do a room search. We'd have had more problems than just Hulda's apiary flu by now if there were more animals in the building. And we'd have noticed litter boxes when the cleaners were in their apartments. Speaking of which, I wonder why the cleaners didn't notice the cat hair in Dottie's apartment?"

"Good thought. Did she cancel cleaning services?"

"I'll look into it. Regardless, thanks for taking care of this for me, Peter. I don't know about doing any further investigation. I'll put a note in her file after I have a quick chat with her, reminding her of the no-pet policy. Unfortunately, I will have to issue a warning to her that any further infractions of the rules could result in eviction. Dottie's a reasonable person. She'll be upset, but I know she'll comply with the rules in the future."

I walked past the entryway and mailboxes on my way back to my office. The voice that called out to me was so soft I barely heard it. Miriam Millam, one of the cooks, was gesturing for me to come to the dining room. Suspecting there had been some meal complaint; I reluctantly followed her to a back corner.

"Where's Wendy?" I asked, scanning the empty dining room. "She's always doing a crossword puzzle this time of the day."

"I haven't seen Wendy much since she's been back from maternity leave. I think she's turned over a new leaf."

"It's almost as if she became a responsible adult," I quipped.

"I heard you've been asking about the Lafayette Bluff car accident. I knew Elizabeth Eggleston. She dated my older brother during their junior year."

Caught off guard, I had to refocus my thoughts. "What was she like?"

Miriam shrugged. "Beth was kind of a mess then. Her boyfriend died, like a week before the prom. My brother had just broken up with his girlfriend, so our mom suggested he ask her to go together as friends. Not really on a date. After the dance, they got invited to a party. My brother was going to Bethel College in the fall. He didn't want to lose his scholarships by getting caught drinking. She told him to drop her off at her car."

"She went to the party alone?"

"I don't know for sure, but I think so. She probably motored over there in her little Pinto and partied until dawn."

"Do you know who else might've been there?"

"They were all three and four years older than me, so I wasn't part of their crowd."

"In a police report, one of the other girls said Elizabeth was partying with the hockey players."

Miriam chuckled. "That's a euphemism for screwing the team. Nobody did that, but a lot of girls were accused of partying with the hockey guys."

"Why the hockey players?"

"They were considered one step wilder than any of the other jocks."

I mulled that comment, then asked, "Is there any chance she got together with someone at the party after the breakup?"

"I heard her boyfriend's band played at the party. I suppose she might've talked with one of those guys between sets. I'm sure she knew them all."

"I don't think she'd do something stupid because of a conversation between music sets."

"Beth wouldn't have been the first or last girl to do something after a party they regretted the next day, week, or lifetime."

"But something in that timeframe got her killed and her car pushed over a cliff?"

Miriam paused and stared out of the dining room windows overlooking Lake Superior. "It was the '70s, Peter. There were alcohol and drugs around. She might've seen or done something that got her sideways with someone."

"Do you think Beth could've committed suicide and her body got carried out with the ice?"

Miriam shook her head. "Not in a million years."

"You're very convinced of that."

"Beth was Catholic. Suicide is a mortal sin."

“Not even if she was distraught about the death of her boyfriend?”
“Not even that.”

Chapter 13

I spent Friday afternoon with Brian, Sparky, Madeline, and Paula. We hid strings of LED lights behind the shelves, and Brian installed a remote switch to turn off the library's main lights and flicker the LED lights. Sparky talked to Pastor Olafson about using the church window, and he set up his projector in a classroom window directly across the street from the library. In the daylight, the image was barely visible, but Sparky assured me it would be perfect after sunset. After that, he set up a microphone in the library so he could hear Madyson calling out to Anna and arranged for his computer-modified voice to play over the library sound system.

After testing all the special effects, we met next to the library desk. "I think we're all set for tonight," I said.

Madeline was enthusiastic about all the technology. "This is so much fun! Can we leave all of this in place for a children's program?"

Sparky shook his head. "I promised the pastor I'd clear all my gear out of the church before Sunday morning.

"Okay, we'll see you all tonight," Madeline said.

"You won't see us at all," Sparky replied. "You'll just see our handiwork."

* * *

As I drove through town, I remembered my conversation about The Secret Owl Society. I made a detour to the barbershop and found Bruce reading a newspaper while sitting in his barber chair. He looked up when I walked in and set the newspaper aside.

"You're about a week early for your usual cut, Peter."

"It was a slow afternoon, so I decided to slip out for a trim."

Like most barbers, Bruce was a master of small talk, chatting about things happening in town while combing and clipping. "I love your nature photography," I said during a break in the discussion. "A friend told me it's difficult to get a picture of a Saw-Whet owl. Have you ever taken one?"

Bruce turned the barber chair so I was facing his cash register, and he pointed to a photo mounted next to a cabinet. "That's what they look like."

"Was that taken locally?"

Bruce chuckled. "Nature photographers are secretive when it comes to revealing where we take our photos."

"It appears you caught him with a camera's flash."

"That's really tricky. First, you have to find his general location based on his call. Then, I use a flashlight to spot him in the tree. If I'm lucky, and if the owl is patient, he'll sit still until I get my camera up, focused, and get the picture taken."

"You must spend hundreds of hours to get one photograph like that."

Bruce chuckled. "Try thousands of hours and hundreds of blurry shots of owls flying away."

"I've heard Saw-Whet owls hang around the rivers when the smelt are running." Bruce kept clipping but stopped talking. "I suppose you've heard I've been trying to find out what was stolen from the library table."

"Yeah, someone mentioned you'd found an old tape recording."

"It's a recording of The Gold Rush playing their hit song, 'Beth.'"

"You're mistaken, Peter. Their song was 'Barb,' not 'Beth.' Cliff Silver wrote it to his wife."

"This version was to 'Beth' and the singer wasn't Cliff Silver."

"A song to Beth, sung by someone other than Cliff?"

"Years ago, someone told me the band had a keyboardist who sang." Bruce closed his eyes for a moment, then said, "Kenny Donaldson."

"What happened to Kenny? Did he drop out of the band?"

Bruce glanced at the Saw-Whet owl picture, then back at my reflection. "He drowned when the guys were smelting on the Lester River. He was probably liquored up and lost his footing."

"I don't suppose you were taking owl pictures when that happened?"

"No."

I always knew Bruce as a straight shooter, and while I didn't want to just accept his "no" as the final answer, I struggled to figure out how to get him to talk further. I decided to just change the subject. "Bruce, how long have you been cutting hair here at Two Harbors?"

"Oh, about 60 years, Peter. I took over for my father in 1966. I expected one of my sons to take over the shop, but none of them have had the talent or interest in barbershop mastery. They decided to go blue collar on me and open up an HVAC shop instead."

"'Blue collar?' You don't consider cutting hair a blue-collar profession?"

"No, Peter. Hair cutting is an art form. Sure, you can spend years in school learning new ways to part hair and to try all the fancy new ways of trimming but cutting someone's hair just right or having a small child in your chair getting his first haircut, that's a calling, Peter. No collar about it."

"Kind of like photography, then. You're an artist in both your profession and your hobby. That's something, Bruce."

"And just like in cutting hair, I learn all kinds of things when people are in this chair, and I learn all kinds of things out there photographing birds. People are willing to talk when they're in nature, Peter. If you're looking for a plot against Kenny, you're barking up the wrong tree. No, I wasn't photographing owls when Kenny died, but I was out smelting. Had my biggest haul that night. I saw Kenny drinking. I saw his bandmates drinking, and I watched them fall into the river together. I watched as the boys got out of the river laughing and thought I saw all four of them. It wasn't until the next day that I realized Kenny hadn't been one of the group I'd seen getting out of the water. And the fact that my eyes deceived me that night has haunted me to this day. And that's all I have to say about that."

"Thank you for that, Bruce. And thank you for my haircut, $20 as usual?"

"Yup."

* * *

After supper, I was preparing to leave for the library. Jeremy stopped me at the door. "Can I go with you to the séance?"

I looked at Jenny, who shrugged. "I don't see why he couldn't go. You've explained all the special effects, so it's not like he'll have nightmares."

183

There were people milling around outside the library when I parked in the Lutheran church's lot. I wondered if Madeline had locked the doors until closer to the planned séance. As we crossed the street, I saw a pile of placards mounted on hockey sticks.

We were accosted at the library entrance by one of the Svenska Gotters. "There's going to be a heathen ceremony. For the sake of your souls, turn around now."

"I think our souls are okay," I replied, pushing Jeremy ahead of me. The library was half-filled with people I didn't recognize, which gave me hope for a successful turnout despite the protesters.

Madeline rushed over to me. "You made it through the protesters?"

"Yes. Are they going to be a problem?"

Madeline steered me to the steps where we were away from the crowd. "These people think the protesters are part of the show."

I looked at the group of people who were chatting and laughing while milling around the lobby. "It's a better turnout than expected."

The streetlights came on, and anticipation was building among the crowd. I saw Sherry and the medium, Madyson, approaching. Across the street, Meg Cochran parked in the church lot, then stood next to her car, considering the protesters, who'd taken up their placards and were now marching in front of the library.

Madyson raced past the protest, but Sherry was confronted and counseled by a church member. I patted Jeremy's shoulder. "I've got to run outside for just a minute. Stay here close to Ms. Jarvis. Okay?"

"Sure. Whatever."

Sherry had pushed past the angry protester, but her face was flushed, and she stared at her feet as if afraid to meet the eyes of the remaining picketers. I held the door open for her as she passed. "Are you okay?"

Sherry paused and frowned. "It depends if you consider eternal damnation a real thing or not."

"Ooh. That's bad."

She nodded. "I think this may be the icing on top of the nude modeling cake."

Meg Cochran stormed across the street as a news van double-parked near the Methbyterian Church. I cut Meg off just before she got to the protesters. Taking her elbow, I steered her toward the library emergency exit.

"What the heck do you think you're doing, Peter?" Meg asked as she pulled her elbow free from my grip.

"I'm keeping you from ruining the best advertising we could possibly get for our ghost tours."

"What?" she snapped.

I pointed to the news crew who had deployed from the white van with the logo of a Duluth television station. "The protesters called the television station. They're going to record a broadcast from here, and everyone in northeastern Minnesota will know about the library and lighthouse ghost tours."

Sparky wandered out of the Lutheran church and started a conversation with the blonde TV reporter. "You're the fire chief, right? Didn't I interview you during the Newt protest?" Sparky straightened up and put on his best professional look. "Yes, I respond to all city emergencies."

"What's happening here?" the reporter asked, pushing a microphone into Sparky's face as the cameraman took a position so the protesters were captured in the background of his shot.

Sparky stared at the protesters dramatically, then turned to the blonde. "Well, the library is haunted, and we've brought in a medium to talk to the ghost, hoping to get her to move on."

"You're doing an exorcism?"

"I don't think we want to get rid of her. I think the city would like it if she stayed around but moved somewhere less...prone to fires and book damage."

"You said, 'her.' Do you know who the ghost is?"

"We do! The ghost is Anna Hansen, the first Two Harbors librarian."

"Where would you like her to go?"

Seeing the news crew talking to Sparky, the protesters started chanting, "No ghost. No séance."

"Well, Anna was a devout Danish Lutheran. We're hoping she'd take up residence in the Norwegian/Danish Lutheran church." As he spoke, Sparky pointed to the Lutheran church immediately across the parking lot. "As a second choice, we thought she might go to this Swedish Lutheran Church."

Looking confused, the blonde asked, "Two Harbors has two Lutheran Churches that share a parking lot?"

"It makes a lot of sense. There isn't a lot of parking around here, and they stagger their services, so the Swedes are cleared out before the Norwegians and Danes show up."

The blonde nodded, even though Sparky had totally glossed over the issue of side-by-side Lutheran churches. "Who are the protesters?"

"They're jealous Methbyterians who think it's immoral to displace the ghost from the library. They're trying to stop the séance."

"Methbyterians?"

"The Presbyterians and Methodists merged. Neither could accept the full conversion to the other sect, so they call themselves Methbyterians now."

I pointed to my watch, hoping to get Sparky ready to produce the ghostly images.

He nodded and gestured to me. "Why don't you follow Peter into the library. You can film the séance."

The blonde turned to me before I could dash away. "What's your last name, Peter, and how are you involved in this exorcism?"

"I'm not really involved other than...helping Sparky," I replied, carefully evading the "last name" question.

"Can we film the exorcism?"

"I don't see why not." I led the broadcaster and cameraman past the protesters and into the library. With the news crew gone, the protesters stopped chanting and huddled.

"This is Madeline, our librarian," I said, as the cameraman got set up. "I think our medium is ready to start." I made a *get-started* gesture to Sherry and she tapped Madyson's shoulder.

"Everyone, gather around the round table," Madyson ordered. "Those standing, please form circles around the table and hold hands."

People shuffled around, most grinning and chuckling about the cheesy drama.

As the room grew quiet, our medium bowed her head and called out, "ANNA, CAN YOU HEAR ME?"

As she called Anna a second time, I texted Brian, "Showtime!" I was starting a text to Sparky when the lights went out and the crowd gasped. I walked to the light switch and flipped it up and down dramatically. Some of the crowd smiled, others looked concerned.

"ANNA, are you with us tonight?" When Sparky's image failed to appear, she asked, "Can you give us a sign?"

The LED lights flickered behind the bookcases, and the crowd's response varied from chuckles to gasps. I looked at Jeremy, who was holding Madeline's hand while standing in the outermost circle of people. He was grinning...right until a row of books fell off an upper shelf deep in the library. The thumping books caused most of the audience to flinch and look into the dark bookshelf area.

Unhappy over the prospect of damaged books, Madeline glared at me. I shrugged and signaled it wasn't my doing.

Sparky finally responded, and the ghostly image of an old woman appeared on the window. The people facing the window mostly gasped, causing everyone to turn. As they looked, Sparky's computer-modified voice came over the sound system. "Why have you summoned me?"

The medium threw her head back and said, "We're here to ask you to leave this library. Go on to your eternal resting place."

"NO!" Sparky said, as the ghostly image raised her right arm. "I am the librarian, and I'm not moving to the Swedish Lutheran Church."

Somewhat stumped by that unscripted response, the medium asked, "Why not?"

"I'm Danish! My last name is spelled H-A-N-S-E-N. I won't move over to the Swedes who spell their last name H-A-N-S-O-N."

I looked at Sherry, who gave me a 'what on earth is going on' look. Madeline was staring at me, too. I shrugged.

Before the medium could gather her thoughts and suggest an alternative, Sparky's voice moaned, then hissed, "Be gone, all of you. Leave me with my books, where I belong."

The apparition disappeared from the window. The crowd, who'd been silent, started chattering. Some started clapping, and the applause rippled through the room as the lights came on.

The man nearest to me smiled and said, "That's the best sideshow I've ever seen. Is there a donation basket here?"

I pointed to a box near the exit. "For anyone feeling generous, there's a donation box next to the door." People filed past me, and most stuffed money into the donation box as they passed. Meg smiled at me as she passed, then stopped on the sidewalk where the protesters were packing up.

With the crowd gone, the blonde reporter stepped over to Madeline and held the mic in front of her. "How did you arrange all of this?"

Madeline glanced at me, and I shook my head. "Anna has been haunting us for about a hundred years. I guess she decided she doesn't want to leave."

From somewhere in the back of the room, a very large book fell to the floor with a smack that echoed for several seconds. We all jumped, and the blonde broadcaster looked rattled. She turned to the cameraman and nodded. "And that ends tonight's broadcast from the haunted Two Harbors Library."

After the lights came on, Jeremy raced through the bookcases to see who had created the sound effect. He reappeared as the cameraman shut down his gear. Sidling up to me, he said, "Dad, there's no one there."

Paula, the library assistant, had followed him. When she returned, her face was ashen. Reinforcing Jeremy's observation, she said, "Really, there is NO ONE there."

Madeline leaned close to me. "How did you do the book things? Is Brian doing that?"

"We didn't *do* any book things."

"Then, how?"

"I have no idea."

Meg spoke to the blonde news reporter while the cameraman packed away his gear. I couldn't hear what was being said, but the blonde nodded emphatically, then typed something into her iPad.

After they left, Brian emerged from the utility room and joined Meg, Madeline, Paula, Jeremy, and me. "How did it look, Doc?"

"The lights were great and the spooky voice over the speakers was pretty good."

"How did you make the books fall?" Jeremy asked.

Looking confused, Brian asked, "What books?"

"At the start, a bunch of books fell off a back shelf. At the end, someone dropped a dictionary on the floor, making a big smash."

"I had nothing to do with that."

Meg's mind was elsewhere. "I spoke to the reporter about tomorrow night's high school concert. She texted her producer about the protest and that they may be back."

"What concert?" Madeline asked.

"The Gold Rush, a 1970s band, is doing a reunion concert at the high school."

Meg nodded. "Yes, and the Svenska Gotters are planning to picket in protest of the suggestive lyrics in the band's songs."

Suspecting I knew the answer, I asked, "How did the protesters find out about the concert and objectionable lyrics?"

Meg grinned. "A little mouse might've slipped that information to them after the séance."

Sparky rushed into the library, waving his cell phone. "I'm on the news!" He stood in the middle of our group and held out his phone. The blonde was featured, with the protesters in the background. "We're broadcasting from the Two Harbors Public Library, where a local religious group is protesting the exorcism of a ghost from the library building. The Two Harbors Fire Chief briefed us on the protest." The blonde held the mic in front of Sparky, who was wearing his most professional, concerned look. I found the spilled spaghetti noodles on his shirt slightly distracting.

The broadcaster listened intently as Sparky explained the ghost and her reluctance to be displaced to the Swedish Lutheran Church.

Meg grabbed my arm and ushered me away from the group. "Thanks for intercepting me before I yelled at the protesters. You were right, we can't buy this kind of publicity."

"I'm concerned that the viewers will think everyone in town is as...colorful as Sparky."

Waving off my concern, Meg smiled. "Tourists love vacationing in places with quirky local people. This might cement our place as a top tourist destination. We'll make the séance an annual event."

"You'll need to talk to Brian, Sparky, and Madyson about their interest in doing this every year."

Meg marched over to the group and interrupted Sparky's retelling of the interview. "This event was absolutely incredible. I'd like to make it an annual event if you guys are willing to help."

Madeline had moved away from the group and unlocked the donation box. As Meg ended her request, Madeline gasped and held up a handful of cash. "There is like two hundred dollars in here! And look, someone put a one-hundred-dollar bill into the box!"

Meg elbowed me and whispered, "Next year, we'll sell tickets."

Chapter 14

After a day of listening to stories about the séance news broadcast, I started for home and left Sherry in charge of transporting the Whistling Pines residents, who'd signed up for the evening concert, to the school. I then needed a plan for supper. After ordering a pizza to go, I finished up my neglected email, picked up the pizza, and rushed home. Jenny was chasing Amy, who'd started stealing the television remote as a way of getting attention. Seeing the pizza box, Jenny sighed. "Pizza sounds good, and Amy loves smearing the sauce all over her face and highchair."

"I knew we wouldn't have time to cook and eat before the concert."

Jenny scooped up Amy and paused. "That's tonight?"

"Seven o'clock."

She glanced at her watch. "Jeremy! Pizza is on the table!" she yelled to divert his attention from whatever electronic device he was glued to in his upstairs bedroom.

I set the pizza box on the table, then took a stack of plates from the cupboard and napkins from a drawer. As I set them out, I commented. "I'm a little concerned about the concert. Ginny Johnson's family has been trying to make sense of the genealogy she's been sharing with them. She sometimes seems totally lucid and confident in what she's saying. The next time they see her; she's telling them something that conflicts with what she previously said."

"That's the nature of dementia," Jenny explained. "Her reality changes from day to day. It's difficult for the family and my staff. We all know her husband has been dead for ten years. Yesterday she reminded us about his imminent return from work and the need to set a place for him at the dinner table. Today she was weepy because she was convinced his funeral was this afternoon."

"This whole thing with the Canadian, who claims to be her nephew, is very confusing for her. She obviously doesn't recognize the man, so she assumes he's a stranger. He's been showing her pictures of his mother and then shows her the test results from his online DNA test. She has no idea what DNA is, much less how it explains that he's her nephew."

"I feel sorry for both Ginny and the Canadian. He's trying to deal with the discrepancy between the father who raised him and the DNA that says otherwise. Ginny is trying to be helpful, but I don't believe half of what she tells him."

"Yeah, distilling the bits of reality from Ginny's evolving stories is challenging. The DNA is definitive, although Ginny doesn't understand that."

Jeremy's feet pounded down the stairs, and he swung into his chair. "Did you get one with sauerkraut?"

"No. No one is interested in trying a sauerkraut pizza."

"Jacob Stone says it's awesome. Most of the others agree."

"The kids might be lying to you, so you'll try something that's terrible. Your friends might be playing a trick on you."

Jeremy stood and slid a wedge of pizza onto his plate. "What's the green stuff?"

"Olives."

He immediately peeled back the cheese topping and started picking off all the olives.

"I thought you liked olives on your pizza?"

"I don't like them *on* my pizza. I like them *with* my pizza. I'll eat them for dessert."

"We've got to leave in about fifteen minutes for the concert at the high school."

"I'm not going."

I stopped with a slice of pizza halfway to my plate. "We're all going."

"Stones aren't making Jacob go to the concert."

"I don't believe that. And you're going whether the Stones are there or not. End of discussion."

"Fine."

Jeremy was grumpy through dinner, and Amy made a mess. I was also grumpy by the time we got out of the house, ten minutes later than I'd hoped. The high school parking lot was nearly full, and people were threading their way through the parked cars to the front doors.

Although Meg said there would be protesters, I was shocked to see what appeared to be the entire Svenska Gotter congregation chanting and waving signs in front of two news vans. "Who is protesting?" Jenny asked as we got closer to the school building.

"It's the Svenska Gotters." As we approached the doors, I read one of the signs, *No Obscene Music*. "The Svenska Gotters think some of the band's lyrics are...suggestive."

Jenny stopped. "Like inappropriate for my children?"

"It'll go over their heads. You know, like climbing the stairway to heaven is about someone's evening of..." I realized Jeremy was suddenly interested in what "Stairway to Heaven" meant. "Someone's romantic evening."

Grimacing, Jeremy said, "Dad. I don't want to listen to songs about romance. Yuk."

"You're sure?"

I quickly thought through what I remembered of the band's song list. "I'm pretty sure we're okay. Unless they slip in a song I don't recall."

"I'm trusting you on this. If there is something inappropriate, you're the one who will explain it to..." she nodded to

Jeremy, who was now distracted by the protesters.

Sparky walked out of the school and scanned the crowd as if looking for someone. He spotted us and rushed over. "Have you seen Wendy?"

"Not recently. What's up?"

"Cliff Silver asked her to sing backup for them. She hasn't shown up yet, and they're tuning their guitars."

"Sorry, I can't help you."

We walked past the protesters, and a woman I'd seen around town glared at me. "This is the devil's music."

Jeremy looked concerned, but I urged him through the line of protesters and into the school. "Dad, why did she say this is the devil's music?"

"There are people who want to censor what other people can read and hear. I think it's up to us to decide what reading and music choices we make. If there's something we need to discuss about this music, or even a book that uses bad words, you and I will talk and decide why it's good or bad. I'm not going to censor what you read."

Jenny listened to us and leaned close to my ear. "Good one, Dad."

* * *

The auditorium/gymnasium had terrible acoustics, and the room echoed with the sound of folding chairs sliding across the floor, children yelling, and several hundred adult conversations.

Deb Stone waved to us and gestured to empty chairs next to their family. Kerry, who felt the police chief needed to sit at the end of the row in case of an emergency, stood so we could pass. As I slid by him, he said, "I really hope this is going to be quieter than the concerts in the park."

I glanced at the gray-haired musicians on stage, tuning their instruments. "I think those guys are past their head-banging, guitar-smashing days."

Kerry glanced at the Whistling Pines group seated in a back corner. "Yeah, the days of their adoring fans screaming and flashing their breasts have probably passed."

Sherry Vogel waved at me, which made me wonder how she was dealing with the Svenska Gotter protest. Her father was their pastor. He was unhappy with several of her life choices, including her job at Whistling Pines.

I stopped halfway between Deb and Kerry. Knowing Deb heard his comment because she was grinning, I glared at him. "Why would you even kid about something like that?" I waved to the Whistling Pines group. "You're just yanking my chain, knowing I'll be paranoid about what my seniors might do."

"Is Alma in that group? Is she going to do her Ava Gardner impression?" Kerry asked.

On several occasions, Alma had shown up in a mink coat, as Ava Gardner had in the 1950s. Ava had surprised Frank Sinatra by flashing him on his birthday. Alma had recreated that scene most recently at a Halloween costume party and a bachelor party.

I chose to ignore Kerry's comment and continued to edge past Deb. She whispered, "Kerry's worried about tonight." She moved over one chair so I could sit next to Kerry.

"Why are you worried about tonight? Four old guys are playing. Half of the audience are senior citizens. What could possibly happen?"

The burned side of Kerry's face was toward me, so I couldn't read his expression. He stared at the stage where the band members were tuning their instruments. "Intuition."

Brian Johnson came rushing from the direction of the stage, anxiously searching the crowd. Seeing Kerry, he nearly ran to us. "Chief, we need you backstage."

I expected Kerry to jump up and follow Brian down the aisle. Instead, he asked, "What's wrong? Did someone object to one of your tuba jokes?"

"This is serious. Peter, you'd better come along, too."

Kerry rose slowly, then looked at me. "I can hardly wait to see which band crisis we're being roped into."

Jenny and Deb gave me a questioning look. I shrugged and pointed toward an open door next to the stage.

Once backstage, Brian led us to the Canadian man who'd been researching his DNA with Ginny Johnson. "I think Peter already knows Perry Endicott. Perry, this is Chief Stone. Tell them what you told me."

Perry looked like he'd been deflated. He glanced around as if he were trying to find someone, then leaned close to Kerry. "My mom is here."

"Your mom?" Kerry asked.

"Yes. She drove down from Kenora. I think she's planning to make a scene."

"What kind of scene?" Kerry asked. "A bunch of old rock and roll performers are putting on a reunion performance. Is she one of the Svenska Gotters?"

"She's planning to tell Cliff Silver that he's my father."

Kerry sighed. "Is that true?"

"She said it's true. The DNA shows I have Megchelson male genes. She used to live in Two Harbors when they were teens. Cliff got her pregnant, and she moved to Canada to raise me. She didn't want me to be a rock star's kid."

I put my hand on Kerry's shoulder before he replied to that. "What's your mom's name?"

"Beth Endicott."

"Her maiden name?"

Perry nodded. "She doesn't tell anyone her maiden name, but I know it was Eggleston."

Brian had been watching the stage until he heard the name. "Your mother is Elizabeth Eggleston?"

"Yes. Is that a problem?"

Kerry took Perry's elbow and steered him to a remote corner of the room, away from the stairs leading to the stage, with Brian and me a step behind. "Your mother disappeared fifty years ago after a car accident."

"Um, okay."

"The police thought she was dead."

"She's going to be here tonight to collect."

"Collect what?" Kerry asked.

"She didn't say. She just said she was going to tell Cliff Silver he was my dad, and to 'collect.'"

"Have you seen her tonight?" Kerry asked as he punched numbers into his cell phone.

"Not here."

"What does she look like?" Kerry asked.

"Kind of grayish hair. Medium height. Average weight. She's probably wearing jeans and a sweatshirt."

Kerry stepped aside and started a conversation with the police dispatcher. I heard him say, "We have a situation at the high school. Send everyone."

Perry looked at Brian and said, "I don't think she brought her gun across the border."

"What kind of gun?" I asked.

"She owns a goose hunting gun. I don't think she brought it."

"What makes a shotgun a goose hunting gun?" I asked as Kerry rejoined us.

"It shoots ten-gauge 3 ½" magnum buckshot shells. It'll kill a goose at seventy yards."

"Whoa!" Kerry said. "What did I miss?"

Perry looked stricken. "I really don't think she'd bring her goose gun across the border."

"That's it!" Kerry declared. "I'm cancelling the concert!"

"You can't cancel the concert," Perry begged. "This might be the only time I get to see my biological father perform."

"If your mother kills him, it'll be the last time anyone sees him perform. Worse yet, there are a couple hundred other people in the building who could be hurt."

A woman with jet black hair raced off the stage and down the steps to us and hissed, "You idiots have to shut up. They're starting the first set."

"Are you Elizabeth Eggleston?" Kerry asked.

"Who in hell is Elizabeth Eggleston and what has she got to do with you bozos making a racket backstage?"

Kerry tried to push past her, but she grabbed his arm. "Hold it, cop. You can't go up there. My husband's band is starting to play."

Kerry tried to brush her aside, but she got into his face. "What part of *back off* don't you understand?" She hissed as Cliff Silver delivered a heartfelt dedication to the memory of Kenny Donaldson to the gym.

"I'm pulling the plug on the concert," Kerry said, trying to push the woman aside as the band broke into the chorus of a song I barely recognized.

"Listen, this is my husband's last hurrah. You're not going anywhere near the stage."

"Get out of my way or I'll arrest you!"

Things became very confusing, not in a small part due to the woman pulling out a canister of pepper spray and aiming it at Kerry's face. Being more situationally aware than the rest of the bystanders, Kerry twisted away from the woman and batted her arm aside, which caused the spray to stream across Brian, Perry, and me. I felt like someone had poured liquid lava into my eyes. I fell to my knees and started coughing. During my training with the Marines, we were sent into a small building, which was filled with teargas. This was more painful but didn't cause as much respiratory distress. I felt my way across the floor, trying to reach a wall where I'd seen the janitor's sink.

There were shouts, groans, and swearing behind me. It was all irrelevant to my mission of rinsing out my eyes. Finding the wall, I used my hands to locate the sink, and I twisted the faucet, which squirted heavenly cold water into my eyes. After a few moments, I tried blinking them clear. The burning was still unbearable, so I bent down and continued to flush away the pepper spray while the commotion behind me continued.

I regained my vision and turned to see what was going on. Kerry had lifted the woman off the ground and held her arms as she squirmed and kicked. Brian was on the floor, crawling around and feeling for a wall. Perry leaned against a wall with his hands over his eyes while groaning.

I spotted a fire extinguisher next to the door and lifted it free. After pulling the safety pin, I aimed it at the woman and squeezed just as Kerry yelled, "Don't!"

He was a second too late because the cloud of yellow powder billowed around them, shrouding them like a Lake Superior fog bank. I released the handle, but the cloud of dust hung in the air, obscuring Kerry and the woman, who were both coughing.

I felt Brian grab my pants cuff. "Doc, is that you? Can you help me?"

I helped him stand, then guided him to the sink to flush his eyes. Then I went back to Perry to help him get to the sink when Brian finished. I then turned toward Kerry and the woman. She'd stopped fighting and was now doubled over, coughing. Kerry blinked at me, his eyes white holes in the yellow powder coating his face and torso. He glared at me, shook his head, and then he walked up the stairs to the stage.

The song was ending when Sparky rushed into the room. "What happened?"

"It's a long story. You need to help Kerry stop the concert." I pushed him toward the stage, and he ran up the steps.

The music stopped, one instrument at a time, then Kerry's voice came over the speakers. "We have a minor problem with the production. The concert is over. Everyone, please leave through the nearest exit."

Kerry huddled with Sparky, Wendy, and the musicians on stage, then led them toward the stairs. A county deputy rushed into the room, looked at the powdery mess and Perry, still curled up against the wall. "What in hell happened here? Where's the Chief?"

I pointed toward the steps. "He's clearing the stage."

"Peter, what's going on? Half the cops in northern Minnesota are on their way here."

"We think a woman is planning to kill the band's lead singer."

The deputy looked around and saw the bossy woman still coughing and trying to catch her breath. "Her?"

"No, a different woman. She has gray hair, an average build, average height, wearing a sweatshirt and jeans."

"You are kidding, right? You just described half of the audience. The other half are men."

"She might be carrying a ten-gauge goose gun."

"Whoa. That'd do a number on a goose or a guy."

The deputy keyed his mic and relayed the information about a woman carrying a shotgun to the other responding units as Kerry guided the band down the steps.

"Chief, what do you need me to do?" the deputy asked.

"Get everyone out of the auditorium. Then, tell every responding unit to report if they see a woman carrying a shotgun anywhere around the school."

Brian's eyes had apparently cleared, and he helped Perry at the sink. The bossy woman, also covered in yellow powder, was talking to the band.

Kerry took me aside. "Shelter in place until I come back for you."

"And if the woman with the shotgun shows up, what am I supposed to do?"

"Try to calm her down."

"Right. I'm not trained in hostage negotiation, and I must've missed the incident de-escalation memo."

"I really don't need a smartass right now. Just deal with it. Okay?"

Realizing how stressed Kerry was, I took a breath and nodded. "Okay."

When Kerry opened the auditorium door, Sherry rushed past him and stopped as she took in the scene. "Peter, is there something I can do to help?"

"Are the residents safely out of the auditorium?"

"Yes, they're in the van."

"What's going on outside?"

"The Svenska Gotters are trying to convert the fleeing crowd. Dad is telling everyone the obscene concert was stopped by God's will and that they should all repent because the day of reckoning is at hand."

"What?"

"You know how my dad is. He seizes every opportunity to proselytize."

"Is he causing problems for you?"

Biting her bottom lip, Sherry shook her head. "He thinks I'm going to hell, so he's kind of given up on me."

Shaking my head, I guided Sherry away from the band. "I'm sorry about your dad. Take the residents back, then go home. We'll talk in the morning."

Chapter 15

The noise in the gym died out as we waited backstage. Wendy broke away from the band and walked to me.

"Peter, your eyes look like you've had the mother of all crying spells."

"Brian and I got hit with pepper spray."

She glanced at Brian, then noticed the fire extinguisher and yellow powder. "Was there a fire?"

"It's a long story."

Sparky joined us and put his arm over Wendy's shoulders. "Honey, we should relieve my mom. She probably thinks we've abandoned her with Blaze."

"We're supposed to shelter in place here until Kerry returns to tell us it's safe to leave."

Wendy pushed Sparky's hand off her shoulder and frowned at him. "Your mother is just fine. We told her we were going to hang out with the band after the concert. She doesn't expect us home until midnight."

The deputy sheriff checked on us and reassured me that my family was safe and on their way home.

Sparky was close to wringing his hands. "Mom probably heard the sirens and is worried. Lend me your phone so I can call her."

"Use your own phone."

"I left it with Mom. She doesn't have a cell phone…"

"Chill!" Wendy snapped. "We're adults. Your mother is okay. The band is going to party at the hotel, and we're going with them."

Sparky glanced at the band members who were huddled together. Perry was gesturing emphatically, making me think he was revealing his secret. Almost on cue, the woman covered in powder shrieked. "YOU NEVER TOLD ME YOU HAD A KID!"

Cliff Silver cringed. "I didn't think…"

"I guess you didn't think!" The woman spun and stuck her finger in Perry's nose. "How old are you?"

I couldn't hear the answer, but it was not what the woman wanted to hear. "YOU GOT SOMEONE PREGNANT WHILE WE WERE DATING? UNBELIEVABLE!"

I looked at Wendy. "I'm not sure the band will be partying."

Cliff circled around the group and put his arm over Perry's shoulder, then they drifted to the back corner of the room, away from everyone. The wives of the other band members circled around the irate woman and made supportive noises.

Wendy watched, then shook her head. "What does she expect? He was a good-looking guy who was the lead singer of a popular band. He had groupies."

I whispered, "I don't think that's what his wife wants to hear right now."

Cliff and Perry were both teary-eyed when they returned to the group. Cliff introduced Perry to the band members with the wives watching. As they spoke, Kerry walked into the room. "The parking lot is secure. Let's get you guys back to the motel." He held the door and stepped aside as the band walked past.

Wendy sidled up to the drummer, a bald guy with a graying fringe of hair and a gut that hung over his belt. "Are you guys still planning to party at the hotel?"

The man smiled, accentuating his facial wrinkles. "We've got a case of vodka in my room. I plan to drink like it's 1980 again."

The woman standing next to him shook her head. "Maybe you should party like you were 70 again. You know, have one drink and go to bed at nine o'clock."

I laughed, then paused. "What's your name?"

The woman laughed. "Jocko, he doesn't know your name. He probably hadn't been born when you guys were popular!"

"My stage name was Jocko. I'm Jack London, like the writer."

I waved to Kerry, summoning him to join us. "Have you got a picture of the partial sheet of music from the library on your phone?"

"We're kind of busy…"

"Just pull it up and show it to Jocko."

Jocko looked at the image, then he looked up at Kerry and me. "Where did you find this?"

Kerry shook his head. "No, tell us what it is."

"It's Kenny's original staff paper from when he wrote…" Jocko paused to reread it. "Holy shit! He wrote the song, not Cliff!"

"I've got that," I replied. "But that's the music to your hit song, 'Barb,' right?"

Jocko glanced at the band who'd walked past us, then whispered, "Don't show this to Silver's wife. Barb will literally kill him. And if anyone at the label knew, Cliff would be in deep shit."

"My family left with the car. Can I catch a ride on your tour bus?"

I heard one of the wives snort. Jocko started to laugh, which rippled through the band and wives. "There's no 'tour bus.' Other than Cliff, we're all driving our personal cars. I had to rent the amps and a trailer to transport them."

"But I thought…"

Jocko leaned close. "Cliff still makes some money off the song royalties. All the rest of us have day jobs." He paused, looking around. "By the way, can you and the fireman help us load up the gear? There are no roadies, either."

* * *

Kerry and one county deputy escorted the caravan to the motel downtown. Cliff pulled his guitar case out of his car. "Hey, guys, bring your instruments in. We'll jam in my room while we party."

Kerry stepped in. "Folks, I'm trying to keep you safe. Can you hustle through the lobby and into your rooms?"

Cliff dismissed Kerry's concerns with a wave of his hand. "We're fine. If Beth shows up, we'll invite her in for a drink. It'll be like old times."

Cliff's wife rushed forward and got into his face. "If that tramp shows up, you'll kick her butt out of the door. No. *I'll* kick her butt out of the door."

"I'm more worried about her shotgun than her butt," Kerry responded. "All of you, get your butts out of the parking lot and into the motel. NOW!"

The band's lack of urgency was driving Kerry nuts. He and the lone deputy went from band member to band member, trying to get them to focus and move out of the parking lot. A cloud of smoke arose from Jocko's car when Kerry realized he was missing and retrieved him. I smelled the marijuana smoke before turning in time to see Jocko flip the roach of his joint under a nearby car.

Kerry was about an inch from exploding when I stepped between the two of them. "Jocko, go into the motel."

"Keep your hair on, man," he replied as he bent down to retrieve something from the car. When he stood up, he had a baggie of green leaves, probably not tea, and a pack of cigarette papers.

Kerry snatched the baggie from his hand. "I'll take care of this."

Jocko, who'd mellowed during the drive to the motel, due in part to the marijuana, smiled. "That's great. I need a free hand for my drumsticks."

When Jocko retrieved the bags from the trunk of his car, Kerry upended the bag and let the leaves, seeds, and buds fall to the ground. He smiled at me. "Oops."

"You weren't going to write him a ticket, were you?"

"I wasn't going to let him flaunt the grass in my face and not react. Problem solved."

"Not cool," Jocko said as he watched Kerry spread the marijuana on the asphalt with the toe of his shoe.

"Come on," Kerry said, taking Jocko's elbow, "we're going into the hotel."

Jocko's wife, whose gray hair made her look close to seventy, followed behind, carrying convenience store plastic shopping bags of potato chips and other snacks.

With Jocko in the lobby, Kerry returned to the parking lot and scanned the remaining cars for Beth or anyone carrying a gun. Seeing no one, he returned to the lobby where the band was milling around, apparently deciding who had booze, cups, marijuana, and a room large enough to host the party.

Realizing all of the band members only had run-of-the-mill rooms, Cliff approached the desk clerk, who'd been watching the scene with amusement. "Have you got a suite or bigger room we could party in?"

"We don't really have any suites, but there is a meeting room where the Lions and Rotary clubs meet." He gestured to an open door just past the lobby.

"Jocko, grab the booze. The rest of you, set up in the meeting room."

Kerry glared at me, so I whispered, "What's wrong?"

"There might be a crazy woman wandering around. I want them all tucked safely into their beds with the doors locked."

"I don't think that's happening. I've been where they are. They're swept up in the moment and ready to perform. They won't be able to sleep for hours, so they're going to play songs, drink, and laugh. Remember, this is their reunion."

Kerry blew out a breath. "Who set this up? Is there a producer or someone who sold tickets? I'm going to bill him for concert security."

"Perfect! Watch the door while these guys get set up."

"Peter, I was being facetious. This is NOT perfect. I would arrest the producer, or whatever he's called, if I knew who he was."

Deb Stone walked into the lobby, saw Kerry and me talking, and joined us. "What's going on?"

I nodded toward the meeting room where the guitar and bass were tuning up to the organ. "The band is having a jam session."

Deb's eyes lit up. "Really? Can we watch?"

Kerry rolled his eyes. "This is not exciting. This is a royal pain in the butt."

Deb put her hand on Kerry's arm and peeked past him into the meeting room. "This is better than having a backstage pass to a concert. This is the after-concert party."

"You have no idea what it's like to have a backstage pass to a concert."

Deb smirked. "I haven't been married to you my entire life. I was a teenager once."

"Really? You went to... Which band? What happened? Tell me you didn't..."

"Easy, dear. I was a good Lutheran girl. There's no way I was going to behave like a lovestruck groupie."

Kerry let out a sigh of relief. "Fine. Go in and watch them. I'll keep an eye on the door."

The elevator door opened, and Jocko stepped out carrying a cardboard liquor case. He nodded toward the elevator. "Hey, cop! Can you grab the orange juice, ice, and glasses?"

"I am NOT your gofer."

Jocko turned to me as he blocked the elevator door with his foot. "Would you give a guy a hand?"

Wendy was looking over Cliff's shoulder at music he'd spread on a conference table. He was pointing out something, and Wendy nodded as he explained.

Satisfied with what she saw, Wendy looked up and spotted Deb Stone. "Hey, Deb! Come over and sing with me like you did at Hugo's."

A smile spread over Deb's face as she stood. She glanced back at Kerry as she approached Wendy. He was scowling, but didn't try to stop her. The two women whispered back and forth, with Deb nodding and smiling as they paged through the music.

Jocko's wife scooped ice into glasses, while the bass player's wife poured orange juice and vodka into the glasses. Cliff's wife distributed the drinks to the band members and their wives, including Wendy, Deb, Sparky, and me. Deb picked up her phone and appeared to be texting someone. She took a selfie with Cliff in the background, then set her phone aside.

Cliff played a chord sequence that sounded like something I recognized from Tom Petty and the Heartbreakers. He nodded to Jocko, who started beating out a rhythm with his drumsticks on a conference table.

"She's a good girl..." Cliff sang the opening of "Free Falling."

Deb and Wendy joined in on the chorus, "And I'm freeeee! Free falling."

I looked at the bass player and keyboard player, who were both playing with their eyes closed. They were *in the zone.*

Cliff slipped into "I Won't Back Down" with Deb and Wendy adding harmony.

When the song ended, Cliff picked up his drink and laughed with the keyboard player. The bassist stepped over, and the three of them huddled together for a moment. Cliff set his guitar aside and hummed a note, then gave a downstroke with his hand.

"There are sights in the southern sky..." and they sang the opening of "The Seven Bridges Road" a cappella. I looked at Deb, whose mouth was agape, in awe of the perfect three-part harmony. Wendy touched Deb's shoulder and motioned for her to follow. They joined the three guys for the second stanza of the song, adding a lovely alto harmony to the guys' tenors. All activity stopped. Jocko's wife had a drink half poured, and she tilted the bottle back. Cliff's wife was carrying a drink to the drummer, and she froze. Everyone knew they were hearing something incredible.

I saw motion at the door and watched Jenny and Sherry edge into the room. Their eyes were glued to the five people singing one of the most incredible a cappella performances I'd ever heard.

When the song ended, Deb Stone had tears streaming down her face. She turned to Wendy, who wore a satisfied smile. Jenny spotted me against the wall and threaded her way around the conference tables and chairs. "Deb texted me. I caught Sherry at Whistling Pines and picked her up."

Sherry joined us. "Are they doing the concert here?"

As we spoke, the desk clerk led a few people, apparently motel guests, into the room.

"They're having a jam session. It's totally impromptu."

Cliff said something to the bassist, who nodded and started a bass riff. The drummer started tapping a rhythm on a table, and the keyboardist played a string of chords. After a few bars, Cliff played the guitar intro to their first hit song, "So Over You." It was a very minor hit, so no one sang along. Even so, the people in the room were rapt. Jocko's wife kept scooping ice and pouring vodka, and Cliff's wife kept handing everyone drinks. Near the end of the song, Cliff's wife approached the desk clerk, who was standing in the doorway beside Kerry. She whispered something in his ear, and he left to do something.

When they finished the song, the bass player kept playing, doing an incredible bass solo, with a familiar sound. Cliff strummed a couple of chords, and the others joined in as they started, "Lyin' Eyes." Deb and Wendy hummed the harmony, then joined in singing the chorus, "I thought by now you'd realize..."

Before the song was over, a young guy carried in a convenience store bag and unloaded bottles of orange juice and tonic. When the song ended, he shouted, "The pizzas will be here in ten minutes!"

Jocko's wife pulled cash from her pocket and held it out to the guy. One of the guests pushed her hand aside and handed the guy $100. "I've got this."

Cliff and Jocko whispered to each other, with Deb and Wendy leaning close to hear the conversation. Cliff turned to Deb and asked something. She nodded emphatically, and Wendy laughed.

"Welcome to our jam session that has become a mini concert. Since you were kind enough to join us, we'd like you to really *join us*. A few years ago, Arlo Guthrie was touring with Pete Seeger. Pete had sung all of the protest songs of the day and decided it was time to step aside and let Arlo sing. Arlo, thinking Pete had already sung any protest song anyone would know, decided to broaden the scope of the concert and invited the crowd to join him in that protest song made famous by the greatest of the protest song singers...Elvis Presley." Cliff waited for the laughter to die, then started picking the opening of "I Can't Help Falling in Love with You" on his guitar. "The girls and I will sing the first verse. If you know the words, join us the next time around."

Cliff nodded to Deb and Wendy, then picked the lead-in and sang, "Wise men say..."

Deb and Wendy completed the three-part harmony. When the verse ended, Cliff picked a few bars, then invited the crowd to join in. The entire room sang, "Shall I stay, would it be a sin..."

I was scanning the crowd as I sang. Thinking the pizzas had arrived, I saw movement behind Kerry at the door. Instead, I recognized Perry, who stood in the door with a gray-haired woman of medium height and build, wearing jeans and a blue Nike sweatshirt. It didn't take a detective to deduce that Elizabeth Endicott had arrived.

Kerry stepped inside the door when the group started singing and smiled as he watched his wife perform. On the other hand, he was unaware that the woman he'd been searching for was standing behind him. I couldn't see anything except a sliver of her through the gathered crowd, so I couldn't tell if she had a shotgun or not. I tried to get Kerry's attention by waving my hand, but he was totally focused on Deb and was singing along.

Pushing my way through the crowd, I reached Jenny and Sherry, who were also totally in the next verse of the song. "Tell Kerry that Beth Endicott is right behind him."

Jenny turned to me. "What?"

"The woman who might have a shotgun is standing behind Kerry. Tell him!"

"What are you going to do?"

"I'm going to...think of something when I get to Cliff Silver."

There was no path to the front. People were shoulder to shoulder, swaying to the music. I edged through, stepping on toes and apologizing as I went. I was halfway to Cliff when the song ended and everyone started clapping. I kept shoving ahead. Trying to reach Cliff to at least warn him about the apparent danger.

"I imagine you'd all like to hear our biggest hit," Cliff announced, bringing a roar and applause in the tiny room. "As I wanted to explain at the dedication concert, my friend Kenny Donaldson actually wrote this song to his girlfriend, Beth, while we lived in Two Harbors. We recorded a demo tape of it, then set it aside for a decade. Our record label needed one more song to complete an album, so we played it from memory, and our producer went wild. The record company liked the song so well, they released it as a single."

Cliff played the opening chords and sang, "Only once in a lifetime..."

The room fell completely silent with Cliff's mellow tenor singing about the love of his life. I heard a commotion near the door, and I panicked, pushing through the crowd.

"Bobby Megchelson!" A woman's voice called from the back.

Cliff stopped playing and looked toward the door, just as I reached him. "Cliff, get down. Beth Eggleston's in the back."

Cliff put his hand on my shoulder, stopping me, as he gazed toward the door. He drew a breath, then waved. People turned to see who he was waving to, then started to chatter.

"Ladies and gentlemen, if I could have your attention!" Cliff shouted. The room went quiet, and everyone turned toward Cliff. He glanced at his wife, who was glaring daggers at him. Then he addressed the crowd. "This is probably going to end my reputation as a songwriter, but as I told you before I started singing, the original lyrics were written by Kenny to his girlfriend, Beth Eggleston, who is standing in the rear of the room."

The crowd turned again. Rather than standing tall and waving back, Beth seemed to shrink. Perry, her son, raised his hand, then pointed at her.

"By the time the song was recorded, both Beth and Kenny were gone, and I was engaged to the love of my life, Barb. I changed the lyrics to her name, and it became a hit. Barb truly is the love of my life, and we've been together ever since then. Much to my surprise, I saw Beth for the first time in...like fifty years." Cliff turned to his wife and said something. With tears in her eyes, she nodded. "I'm going to play the first verse of our hit as Kenny originally wrote it, to Beth. Then, please join me in singing the second verse to Barb, the way it is in my heart."

I looked at the door where Perry had his arm around his mother's shoulders. Her face was buried in her hands, and her body shuddered, as if she was sobbing. As Cliff started singing, I glanced at Barb, who stood next to him with tears streaming down her face while she smiled. I thought to myself, *I guess there's not going to be a divorce after all.*

I stepped aside and stood by Wendy and Deb as we harmonized on the chorus. The bass, drums, and keyboards all joined as Cliff sang the second verse to Barb.

When the song ended, people passed pizza boxes around, and Jocko's wife walked among the partiers with a stack of cups and a bottle of vodka. The drummer's wife was a step behind her with a gallon of orange juice in one hand and two liters of tonic water in the other, filling cups after people were served their vodka shots.

I pushed my way against the flow to the back of the room, where I found Jenny and Sherry talking with Perry and his mother. I stepped next to the chief and whispered, "No shotgun?"

He shook his head. "We're good."

"And you're okay with the band sloshing booze into cups and handing them out to the crowd?"

Turning his back to the room, he replied, "I don't see any booze." He glanced at the parking lot. "I think we might set up outside to do field sobriety tests on people who shouldn't be driving themselves home."

I chuckled, then spotted the Whistling Pines van parked near the door. "I think we can arrange a sober cab for anyone who needs it."

I was surprised when Cliff Silver brushed past me. He walked up to Beth and Perry. I couldn't hear what was said, but he appeared contrite. He hugged Perry, then stood awkwardly in front of Beth. She said something, then wrapped her arms around him.

"I thought you were dead."

Beth sniffled back a tear and wiped her nose with a tissue. "No, just in Canada."

"Why fake your death? I mean, there were options. I offered to pay for an abortion."

Beth shook her head. "I'm Catholic, there's no way I was having an abortion. My parents would've killed me if they'd found out I was pregnant." She shrugged and added, "I thought it was easier to just be dead. Kenny's death destroyed me. Our time consoling each other about his death should have obliterated me; instead, we created the

best thing that's ever happened to me.
Perry."

Cliff pulled Perry into his hug. "You could've told me I had a son."

"No. You were a big star, and I married a nice guy. I'd disowned my entire past."

Epilogue

Brian showed up in my office the next morning with two take-out cups of coffee. "Good morning. I hoped I could catch you away from Hulda and the other rumor mongers." He pulled the door shut behind himself.

"This must be serious; you didn't tell me a tuba joke."

He handed me one of the coffees and sat in my chair. "Did you hear what happened with Cliff Silver and Beth Eggleston after the party broke up?"

"I didn't." As soon as I'd made the comment, I remembered that Brian hadn't been at the motel. "How do you know what happened? You weren't even there."

"It's Two Harbors, there are no secrets." Brian took a sip of coffee. "All future royalties from the hit song are going to Beth. Cliff described that as past due child support. Beth said it'll be a college fund for their grandchildren."

"Are there any royalties from the song? It was a hit long ago; the writer only receives royalties when the song is played."

"Someone took a video of the motel party. It's gone viral. I think Cliff will be on every one of the talk shows doing gut-wrenching human-interest stories. I'm sure the same will be happening to Beth and Perry in Canada. The song will probably be back on the charts again. Funny thing is that even though Kenny actually wrote the song, the fact that Cliff wrote in Barb's name and modified one of the verses makes him an actual writer of the song, and the label won't be on the hook for paying out royalties to Kenny's family."

Brian paused, and his eyes twinkled. "I heard your apiary flu outbreak was a cat allergy."

"I'm amazed anyone outside of Whistling Pines would know that."

"Too bad you're not having a herpes cold sore outbreak. The unemployed clarinet player is a herpetologist."

Pressing my fingertips to my temples I replied, "Brian, herpetologists are not experts in herpes. As I recall, they're into reptiles and amphibians."

"That makes so much more sense. Ellie Ogren told me she'd done her research on spring peeper mating. I had been thinking about peeping Toms. Spring peepers are frogs."

"Don't you need to be at a band practice or something?"

"Not really. If I could be of help with your nanny search, I'd be happy to skip an hour or two of tuba practice."

"I don't have any nanny related issues right now. Go ahead and practice." I turned back to my computer and started catching up on emails.

I was surprised when Jenny walked into my office looking harried. She handed me a list with five names crossed off and three remaining. "Here are the applicants. They're going to be at the house every half hour starting at six. Let me know who you choose."

Dumbstruck, I accepted the list. "I'm choosing the nanny?"

Jenny sighed. "The Department of Health is visiting on Monday. I'm going to make sure our procedures are up to date. After that, I'll coach my evening staff about the visit."

"I'm not qualified to interview nanny candidates. I'll reschedule them."

"You're very perceptive, and based on our phone conversations, I don't think any of the people on the list would be a bad choice. I just need you to talk to them and determine who would be the best fit." Jenny stood, then stopped at the door. "Sparky's planning to be over at six to help."

"I'm interviewing nannies with Sparky? He's clueless." I protested to the empty door.

* * *

Jeremy was working on homework, and I'd just cleared the supper dishes when someone knocked on the back door. Scooping up Amy, I walked to the door just as it opened. Sparky walked in carrying Blaze. "Wendy told me you needed me to help interview nannies."

"If you've got something else to do, I can probably handle this alone," I lied, hoping he'd be happy to be released from the commitment.

"That would be great. We have a fire hall meeting, and I need to be there." He held Blaze out to me.

"I can't watch both Blaze and Amy while interviewing candidates," I protested.

"I can't bring Blaze to the fire hall. Wendy's mom yells at me when I say 'heck' around him. Most of the firemen use stronger language than that."

The doorbell rang at precisely six o'clock. I rushed to answer it while Sparky was still trying to explain why he needed to leave Blaze with me. The woman at the door looked like she'd been ridden hard and put away sweaty. Her heavy makeup failed to completely hide her black eye. She flicked a cigarette butt into the bushes and exhaled smoke over her shoulder. "I heard you were looking for a live-in nanny." Behind her, I saw a beat-up car with several children inside fighting.

I was about to gesture for her to come in when one of the children rolled down the car window. "Mom, Kyle Wayne is peeling your cigarette butts and spreading them on the seats."

The woman's smile disappeared. She turned toward the car and yelled, "Shaddup!" Turning back to me, she tried to force a smile.

"I'm sorry to have wasted your time, but the job was filled this afternoon."

The woman glared at me, then spun on her heels and returned to the fighting children in her car.

Sparky joined me at the door as the woman walked away. "She looked scary."

"I told her the job had been filled."

"Wow, lucky you'd already hired someone. Who is it?"

"I haven't hired anyone. I told a white lie because I could see she wasn't the kind of person we wanted."

Sparky blinked as if he'd never told a white lie. "Oh." Blaze squirmed and then let loose with a juicy fart, followed by squirming and crying. "I don't suppose you have a diaper I could borrow?"

"Amy's got Pull-Ups that are way too big for Blaze."

"I don't suppose you'd like to walk over to our place and change his diaper?"

The doorbell rang again. "I've got to interview the next candidate." I opened the front door as Sparky and Blaze left through the kitchen.

The young woman on the doorstep wore earbuds and put up her finger to stop me while she finished a conversation on her phone. I was intrigued by the lizard tattoo on her neck, multiple ear piercings, and nose ring. "I'm here for the nanny job."

I was about to invite her inside when her phone rang again. Rather than silencing the ringer, she stepped away from me to take the call. After a heated exchange, she turned to me. "Men are thoughtless turds. My boyfriend lost his apartment, and he wants me to find a place." She stopped, looked around the living room as if considering the living conditions for her and her boyfriend, then glanced at Jeremy, who was working on math at the dining room table. "I'm sorry. I can NOT deal with a boy on the edge of puberty. I'm out of here."

She rushed out of the door, almost knocking over Deb Stone. Glancing at the fleeing young woman, Deb asked, "What did you say to scare off that applicant?"

"She apparently doesn't do pre-pubescent boys."

"Ah," Deb replied with a knowing nod. "They do present certain challenges."

"What brings you over?" I asked.

"Jenny asked me to check in on you. She was afraid you might be overwhelmed with the interviews and might appreciate me taking Amy upstairs for a while."

"That would be..." The doorbell rang before I finished the sentence.

Deb took Amy and gestured for me to answer the door. The third, and final, applicant was neatly dressed in khakis and a dress shirt. She smiled and handed me her resume. "I heard you were looking for someone with references."

I scanned her resume and was mildly impressed with her two previous nanny jobs which ended when her employers relocated. "Please come in."

I estimated that she was about thirty and carried an air of confidence along with her professional appearance. I explained our arrangement with Sparky and Wendy, introduced Jeremy, and said a friend was watching Amy upstairs.

"I heard you are a musician."

"I'm not a professional musician. My wife and I work at Whistling Pines. I sometimes play guitar for the residents."

"I heard you at Hugo's, playing with the Gin Fizzes. You're really talented."

"Thank you. I fill in when the Gin Fizzes' guitar player is unavailable."

She reached down to her bag and pulled out a joint and lighter. "Being artistic, you don't mind if I smoke, do you?"

Jeremy glanced at her, then at me, waiting to see how I'd react.

"I do mind. Our interview is over."

The woman looked surprised. "You're a musician. You probably smoke dope and do all kinds of drugs."

I walked to the door and opened it. "Our home is a drug-free zone. Goodnight."

I closed the door, and Jeremy stared at me. "She had a cigarette."

"No, she had a marijuana joint. That's totally inappropriate for a nanny."

Deb walked down the stairs and overheard the end of our conversation. "Really? A woman showed up for a nanny interview and asked if she could light up?"

"Yeah."

"Was she your last interview?"

"Jenny and Wendy had whittled the list down to three, and I've rejected all of them."

"What are you going to do now?"

Jeremy walked to Deb and hugged her. "I wish you could be our nanny. You and Jacob could come over every afternoon. He and I could do homework together and play games when we finished our homework."

I looked at Deb, who seemed as shocked by the suggestion as I was. She tousled Jeremy's hair and said, "Why don't you get ready for bed. Your dad will be up to tuck you in after a bit." We watched Jeremy run upstairs, and Deb turned to me. "Would you consider hiring the police chief's wife as your nanny?"

The suggestion was so outlandish, I was at a loss for words. "Are you serious?"

"I'm bored at home, and I love your kids. You and Jenny are our closest friends, so I'm already like a family member. Why not?"

"I suppose hugging the nanny is inappropriate."

Deb spread her arms. "I think I'll allow this one exception."

Upstairs, the organ played the opening notes of "Over the Rainbow."

Deb frowned. "Was that your doorbell?" She asked as we released the hug.

"How do you feel about organ-playing ghosts?"

"I don't believe in ghosts."

"In that case, the organ plays itself every once in a while. It likes "Over the Rainbow" when good things are happening."

"Huh, like a player piano?"

"Something like that."

"Call Jenny and tell her you've hired someone."

As I took out my cell phone, I asked, "What are you going to tell Kerry?"

"Ever since I married Kerry, I've been a *good officer's wife*. I've hosted coffee parties for the other officers' wives, I've nursed Kerry back from his injuries, and most recently, I've been a good chief's wife. It's my turn to be...just me. Kerry's encouraging me to volunteer at the library and the historical society. He'll be pleased I'm doing something I find fulfilling."

Before I could select her phone number, Jenny walked through the back door looking exhausted. "Deb, did you rescue Peter?"

I gestured for Jenny to join us in the living room. "I'd like you to meet our new nanny."

Jenny's tiredness disappeared, and her eyes filled with tears. "No. Really?"

Deb nodded. "It'll be my privilege."

"You do understand that you'll have to deal with Sparky and Wendy?" Jenny offered.

"Sparky is afraid of me. I've told off a general's wife when she was out of line, so I can deal with Wendy if I need to." Deb paused. "This only works if I can bring Jacob here after school."

"Having the boys occupying each other will make it easier to deal with Amy and Blaze. I think that's a great approach."

* * *

"Ginny?" Jenny and I brought Beth Endicott into Ginny Johnson's room the day after the eventful concert.

"Hi Jenny. Is it time for lunch already? I thought I just had breakfast."

"No, Ginny, it's not time for lunch, you have a visitor."

"Hi, Auntie Ginny."

"Bethie! You haven't visited me in ages. Where have you been?"

Tears streamed down Beth Endicott's cheeks as she sat with her Aunt Ginny, finally reunited after years of hiding.

The End

Dean Hovey is the award-winning and best-selling author of three mystery series. He uses his scientific background, travel, extensive research, and consultants to add reality and depth to his stories. One reader said his characters are like people he'd like to invite over for a beer and discussion.

Dean and his wife split their year between northern Minnesota and Arizona.

Whistling Librarian is Anne Flagge's first book. Anne uses her teaching and healthcare background to create interesting characters and a great plot. Her rural northern Minnesota childhood, surrounded by a colorful extended family, allows her to tap into a deep well of humor and senior experiences.

Anne and her family live in north central Iowa, but her Minnesota roots frequently drag her back to the Northwoods.

Dean Hovey books, published by BWL Publishing

Whistling Pines cozies

Whistling up a Ghost
Whistling Pirates
Whistling Bake Off
Whistling Artist
Whistling Fireman
Whistling Wedding
Whistling Librarian

Doug Fletcher mysteries

Stolen Past
Washed Away
Dead in the Water
Death in Shifting Sands
Devils Fall
Prairie Menace
Down River
Burnt Evidence
Gator Bait
Grave Survey
Dead End Trail
The Last Rodeo
Peril in Paradise
Western Justice
Strung Out to Die
Medora Murder
A Bourbon to Die For

Pine County Mysteries
Killer Secrets
Deadly Mixture
Fatal Business
Taxed to Death
Conflict of Interest
Skidded and Skunked (with D.L. Dixen)

BWL Publishing

bwlpublishing.ca